This book

Children's
POOLBEG

To Eugene and Mai Lambert

BACK OF BEYOND

A NOTE ON THE AUTHOR

Patricia Lynch was born in Cork in 1898. She was educated in Ireland, Britain and Belgium. As a young journalist she wrote an eye-witness account of the 1916 Rising. She wrote over fifty books, mostly for children, published the world over and translated into many languages.

She lived in Dublin with her husband, the writer RM Fox, and died in 1972.

BACK OF BEYOND
PATRICIA LYNCH

Children's
POOLBEG

First published by JM Dent & Sons Ltd, 1966
This paperback edition published 1992 by
Poolbeg Press Ltd
Knocksedan House,
Swords, Co Dublin, Ireland

© Patricia Lynch, 1966

A catalogue record for this book is available from the British Library

ISBN 1 85371 206 X

Cover design by Judith O'Dwyer
Set by Richard Parfrey in ITC Stone 10/14
Printed by The Guernsey Press Company Ltd,
Vale, Guernsey, Channel Islands

Contents

1

The Mysterious Journey

The Brophys' house was in an uproar! Tim Brophy was out in front making sure his car was in perfect order. He stood there, ticking off on his fingers all he would need for the journey to Westport, straight down through Mayo, past Lough Mask and Lough Corrib to Galway City, then right across Ireland to Dublin.

"That's a queer journey," murmured the old grandmother, who was cutting sandwiches for him in the kitchen and listening to the talk going on outside. "But what harm. If he doesn't know his way about Ireland by this time he never will, that's sure. But he does love making a mystery of where he's going."

"Pyjamas," muttered Tim, ticking the list off. "Change of underwear, shirts, collars, socks, handkerchiefs, writing-pad, envelopes, headed notepaper, account book, pens, pencils, razor, soap, comb, hairbrush, toothbrush.

"Now what else can there be?" he wondered, biting his thumb. "I know I have all my trade parcels safe. The rubbish I have to carry! Anyone might think I was off to the North Pole. But when I reach Dublin, that will be the day I'll remember."

Garry, the eldest boy, had been busy polishing the car. Now he stood back, the chamois leather in his hand and smiled up at his father.

"Dad, when will you teach me to drive?" he asked suddenly.

His father's eyes twinkled.

"When you're as big as I am, son," he answered. "Then the poor old dad will sit in the back seat, among the samples, and admire the young lad in front, keeping ahead of everything going the same way. Just you wait and see."

"I suppose you won't tell me what the surprise will be this time?" said Garry even more coaxingly.

"You're right there, me lad! Dead right!" agreed Tim Brophy. "I will not. Go in now and give your grannie a hand with the list of what I'm to bring home. It'll be a long one this time!"

"You won't forget the surprise?" persisted the boy anxiously.

His father put his head on one side.

"That's one thing I won't forget," he promised. "Now let's go inside and see what mischief the women of the family are up to."

"But where are you bound for this time?" Garry asked. "Is it somewhere extra special? You've never made such a fuss before."

His father put his hands on his hips and pursed his lips together as if he were whistling silently. He tossed his head.

"Making a fuss, am I?" he cried indignantly. "Some boys would make a fuss when they see their poor father going off to face the world alone! But have my children any pity for me? Not one of them! Not one!"

By this time they had reached the door of the kitchen where Nuala, the only girl, was helping her grandmother to make sandwiches for her father on the journey.

The old woman cut the bread as thin as she could. Nuala buttered the bread and put in the thick slices of lean ham. Boots, the black cat, sat on a corner of the table purring loudly, swishing his long bushy tail and, now and again, stretching out a velvety white paw.

"Ah, Grannie, do give poor Boots a tiny bit," pleaded Nuala. "He's been so good."

Old Mrs Brophy, who never said no to her granddaughter if she could possibly help, jerked a big piece over to the cat, who seized it and jumped down.

Nuala heard what her father was saying as he entered the room. She ran across and flung her arms around him.

"Oh, Daddy, I do pity you having to go on these long journeys. So does Garry, Danny and Peter. And you know how sorry Gran always is to see you go away. Besides, last night you did say this place was the Back of Beyond, and you didn't know how civilized people managed to live here.

You did say that, didn't you?"

She looked up at him with big admiring brown eyes, for she thought her father was the most wonderful man in the world.

Tim Brophy laughed down at her.

"Did I really say it was the Back of Beyond?" he asked. "Didn't I also say what a lovely little place it was to be coming back to?"

Nuala nodded, shaking her golden brown hair over her face.

"You did," she agreed. "I had forgotten."

Old Mrs Brophy wrapped the sandwiches in a sheet of grease-proof paper, slipped the parcel into a brown-paper bag and gave it to him.

"The coffee is in the vacuum flask in the left-hand corner of the back seat," she told him. "Don't forget now, and buy a bunch of good ripe bananas to keep you going until you're settled in the Dublin hotel. Take care of yourself. We'll miss you. But, sure, you're not going to be away long this time"

"Are you really sorry to see me go?" he asked. "All of you?" He looked round and pretended to be very doubtful.

"You know we are," declared Peter scornfully. "But don't forget what you promised to bring back to me."

His thick red hair was standing on end as usual. His face was smudged. But he stared boldly at his father as if daring him to deny that he had promised anything.

Tim Brophy stared back.

"Did I promise to bring you anything at all?" he demanded. "Now why should I do that? Are you sure?"

"Oh, Daddy!" cried Nuala. "You know you did. You were going to bring a great big engine with a real horn. And you haven't forgotten it will be my eleventh birthday as soon as you do come back, and you did say you'd bring me back the best present I've ever had."

She flung her head back and laughed up at him.

"Did I make these promises, Gran?" he asked, frowning, though his eyes were twinkling. "And did I really call this place the Back of Beyond?"

"You did indeed!" declared Mrs Brophy, folding her arms and trying to look fierce.

"Isn't it terrible," sighed Tim, shaking his head sorrowfully. "Here am I leaving home and going out into the cold world and all I hear is abuse, just abuse!"

The children laughed delightedly.

"Gran never knows how to abuse anybody—you should know that," Garry told him.

"Then you'll stand up for her while I'm away," said his father, smiling.

"Of course I will."

"And you'll take care of the young ones?"

"Don't be tormenting the child," chuckled their grandmother. "You take care of yourself and come back safe and sound. Don't try to pass all the other cars and remember to have your meals at the proper time."

Tim opened his mouth, frowned, shut it again, shook his head laughingly, gave a hug all round, went out of the house quickly, scrambled into the car, blew the horn three times and whizzed down the road. He slowed up at the corner, thrust his head out of the window and murmured "God keep you all!" In another moment he was out of sight.

Grannie Brophy shaded her eyes from the sun's rays as she looked out over Blacksod Bay. She gazed up at the mist-shrouded heights of the Stack Mountains.

"Will it rain tomorrow?" asked Garry anxiously. "Mick Doyle promised to take me fishing if the weather stays fine. As if I cared whether it's wet or fine. But you know what he is—he won't let me go with him if it's the least bit stormy."

The old woman smiled at him.

"And isn't he right, son?" she asked. "You know you're a terrible lad for catching cold, and summer sandals aren't the best footwear for wet days. Your father promised me he'd take you into Sligo as soon as he gets back and buy you a pair of high water-proof boots."

Garry's blue eyes sparkled.

"D-did he really p-promise t-that?" he stammered, almost breathless with delight.

"He did indeed," Mrs Brophy assured him. "And I've a feeling that he won't be away too long—this time."

She looked so serious as she spoke that Nuala

felt anxious. Why was her father coming back sooner than usual? Why was he so mysterious about his journey? She had noticed her grandmother looking at him in a puzzled way as she did when Garry was planning something he didn't want anyone to know. But, somehow, with Garry she always seemed to know.

"Dad's up to something he doesn't want us even to dream about until he tells it himself," Nuala murmured. "And why shouldn't he? Haven't we all our secrets?"

Tim Brophy appeared to be the one man in the district completely satisfied with his job. It took him travelling up and down the country. He kept small shops in scattered little towns supplied with drapery goods for men, women and children. He went to Cork, Dublin and Belfast. Sometimes he crossed to England, and once he had been as far as France.

"What a great traveller he is," thought Nuala proudly. "He has travelled more than anyone else in the village except, of course, Father Clancy, who has been to Rome." The O'Donnells—the whole twelve of them—had gone to America. But they were emigrants and wouldn't be coming back.

Her father had promised to take her and Garry with him when they were a little older. She drew a deep breath.

"I would love to go to Cork," she thought. "I don't mind not seeing London or Paris. Heaps of people have never been anywhere. But Gran says we should see all we can of our own country while we're young and have the time. Of course she's right—she always is!"

Mrs Brophy stood in the doorway, her arms folded, her eyes fixed on that sharp bend in the road where her son and his car had passed out of sight.

"He has something on his mind," she said to herself slowly. "Now I wonder what it is and why he didn't tell me? It's bringing him back earlier than usual. What can it be? Nothing bad I hope."

"Look!" cried Nuala suddenly. "The birds! The great, white, lovely birds!"

She pointed and they stared. It looked like a white jagged cloud blown along by the wind. But there was no wind.

Soon they saw it wasn't a cloud but a group of swans—four big snow-white swans with long graceful necks and outstretched wings beating. They came swiftly, circled slowly and more slowly until, for a moment, they were still with their wings outspread. Then they dropped, but so gently that they hardly made a splash or a ripple as they reached the water. They glided on the surface like proud ships with white sails reflected in the still water.

"Four white swans," murmured the old woman. "That is a sign of great, good luck."

"Oh, the lovely birds!" cried Nuala. "I wish Daddy had been here to see them."

"Maybe they'll still be here when he does

return," said her grandmother.

"I'm hungry," grumbled Danny.

"Thirsty," added Peter.

The two small boys squeezed up to their grandmother. She rumpled their hair and laughed.

"I told your father to make sure and have a good cup of coffee from his flask," she said. "How would you children like some too? It's very comforting."

The two boys stared at her in wonder.

"We never drink coffee!" exclaimed John. "You always said it was only for grown-up people."

The old woman sighed.

"Right enough," she said. "But somehow I need a bit of comforting, and coffee is a great comfort. Besides, I wasn't keeping my mind on the job and I made far too many sandwiches. There's a pile of them on the table. We'll have a picnic lunch and I'll make an omelette for tea. How would you like that?"

"You know, Gran, it isn't anybody's birthday," Garry reminded her.

"But it would be lovely," cried Nuala, "and we can celebrate the coming of the swans."

"Hungry!" sighed Danny again.

Mrs Brophy laughed.

"I never knew such a boy. He must have been born starving!"

"Me too," said Peter, trying to make himself important.

"They're just **two** greedy little beggars," declared

Garry. "They're always hungry or thirsty."

His grandmother looked surprised.

"So you won't try my nice fresh sandwiches," she said. "I thought it would be a treat. And I wouldn't like that big pot of coffee—sweet, milky and piping hot—to go to waste."

Garry laughed.

"Now you're just teasing," he told her. "But it serves me right."

Nuala slipped her hand into Mrs Brophy's.

"And because Daddy's away and we're feeling lonesome, please tell us a story—a lovely long story, that can go on and on and on until he comes back. Please!"

"A story! A story!" shouted the two little boys.

"I'd like that too," declared Garry. "Only let it be a real story, not just a yarn to keep those young ones quiet."

"I'll do me endeavours," promised their grandmother as she closed the door slowly, for she was still looking at the four great white swans.

"They could bring great good luck—but not always," she murmured.

2

Gran Tells a Story

The sun was shining but there was a cold wind blowing down from the north. A rattle like hailstones beat on the two windows. Only this wasn't hail but spray tossed in by the wind.

They were all glad of the fire, not only for the warmth but for the gay, dancing light it flung into the dark corners of the room. Gran Brophy sat at one side in her armchair. The sofa was drawn up at the other. Garry and Nuala each had a corner while Danny and Peter curled down on the rug with the big black cat—called Boots because of his four white paws—between them, purring loudly.

The sandwiches were the best Mrs Brophy had ever made. Her coffee was always as it should be— hot, strong and not too sweet. She sent Garry out to the little cupboard for a dish of small russet apples so that they could chew and chew while she told them the story.

"It's a long, long one," she warned them. "So it won't be finished today or tomorrow either."

"I like long stories," declared Garry, "for then

we have something to look forward to."

"And I must also tell you," went on Mrs Brophy, "that it is very sad."

"Couldn't you make it come happy at the end," pleaded Nuala.

"I can't alter it, Nuala darling, because it's a true story," her grandmother told her. "I suppose the end is really happy. It's the in-between part that is sad. You must put up with that."

"I'll remember," promised Nuala. But she looked mournful.

"Don't you start crying!" ordered Garry. "We promised Dad we wouldn't be miserable while he's away."

"I won't cry whatever happens," said Nuala firmly. "I'll nurse Boots. He'll be a comfort."

Boots was quite willing to be nursed. Garry took out the coffee-pot and the empty sandwich plate so that the sitting-room had the neat look that Gran Brophy liked. The two small boys hugged their knees.

"Please start, Gran," pleaded Danny, "or Peter will be falling asleep."

"I don't fall asleep any more than you do," declared Peter hotly. "Besides, it isn't night time. It's only the middle of the day. We haven't had our tea yet."

"Just listen to that one!" exclaimed Garry scornfully. "He never thinks of anything but eating."

"I'm not hungry," his young brother assured

him. "But I will be if the story doesn't start soon."

"Greedy!" muttered his big brother.

Their grandmother laughed.

"I'd better begin the story at once," she said. "Now listen, children.

"Once upon a time, a long, long time ago—"

"That's the way I like a story to begin," whispered Nuala.

The others nodded.

"In ancient Ireland," continued the story-teller, "there was a king—King Lir. He had four children, three boys and one girl."

"Just like us," whispered Danny, who could never keep quiet.

"Sh!" muttered Nuala.

"Shut up!" muttered Garry.

"Tell us their names," ordered Peter.

"The boys were called Hugh, Fiacha and Conn. The girl was Fionnuala!"

"Like you!" said Peter, looking in amazement at his sister. "That's your full name—Fionnuala!"

"Fionnuala and Hugh were twins," went on Mrs Brophy.

"I'm older than you!" Garry told his sister proudly.

"Now you shut up!" Danny cried.

Gran Brophy smiled. She was used to being interrupted when she began telling a story and she didn't mind, for the children always settled down when they became interested in what she was saying.

"King Lir loved his children, but he was very lonely because their mother was dead. He took them with him to stay at the palace of his cousin Red Bov.

"A great many of Red Bov's friends and relations lived with him and they tried to make King Lir happy again. One of Bov's foster-daughters, Aoife, was so kind and lovely that soon Lir could not let a day pass without spending time in her company, often riding with her.

"Of course he could not stay away from his kingdom for ever, so at last he prepared to go home, and went around Bov's palace saying farewell to all those who had been so kind to him and the children.

"When he came to say goodbye to Aoife he could not bear it, and she wept at the thought of the days without him. At last she agreed to marry Lir, to leave the gay crowded palace of Bov, to go to Lir's solitary fort and be a mother to his children."

Gran Brophy drew a deep breath and looked at the children, who were very quiet and serious. They had heard of cruel stepmothers before—in fairy stories.

"Maybe she won't be like the others," thought Nuala hopefully.

"At first Aoife was very good to the children, and so charming to everyone in the fort, that most of them began to forget King Lir's first wife. But Fionnuala remembered her real mother and often longed for her.

"She was a wise, lovely child and Lir would have hated to leave her when he was journeying round his little kingdom, but he felt she was sure to be happy with her kind, beautiful stepmother.

"While he was away Aoife ruled the fort. She was clever, and made herself so pleasant to everyone that her orders were obeyed without question. Lir was delighted with this new life and went off on his travels feeling perfectly happy and content."

Gran Brophy paused and leaned back in her chair. The children sat up and stared at her.

"You can't stop now!" protested Garry. "I must know what happens next."

"Did she keep on being kind?" asked Nuala doubtfully.

"I don't care if it is tea time," said Danny. "You can't leave us all night without knowing what's going to happen, can you, Gran?"

Mrs Brophy laughed.

"I'll have a little rest, then I'll go on," she told them. "You see I have to remember as I go along and it's quite a while since I heard that story. Besides, my voice does get tired sometimes."

Danny stroked her hand.

"Rest whenever you want to, Gran," he told her grandly. "We've got heaps of time."

"Thanks be for that," she chuckled. "Well, for quite a while Aoife was happy and content when she saw how she was liked and admired by everyone. She saw how Lir made his horses gallop at their swiftest speed when he came in sight of his 'Dún' as they called the forts in those days.

"But Fionnuala grew taller and lovelier every day. Aoife heard the men and women of the dún saying to one another how like her dead mother she was. Slowly Aoife's affection for her step-daughter turned to dislike, which gradually deepened into hatred.

"One day Lir took Fionnuala's face between his hands and, smiling down at her, whispered 'How like your mother you are growing.'

"He spoke so softly that neither he nor Fionnuala guessed anyone overheard. But Aoife, who was passing, heard what he said. Her face stiffened, her eyes flashed, and to keep herself from crying out in anger she had to press her nails into the palms of her hands.

"The next moment she was smiling sweetly as usual. But when she said good night to her young stepdaughter there was no kindness in her voice but a harsh coldness.

"From that time Aoife's hatred of Fionnuala grew until it was very difficult for her to hide this. Lir was so often away that she managed to speak gently and kindly to the girl when the king was at home. But Fionnuala felt the change, and soon it was becoming harder and harder for Aoife to pretend that she had any love for her stepdaughter.

"Winter was coming nearer when Lir set off on his last journey for the year. There was great coming and going at the dún and out beyond the great wall, with men and women carrying to the king's chariot the loads of presents he was taking to his friends and tribesmen. Lir felt very happy, for he was a generous man and delighted in bestowing gifts on those whose friendship he valued.

"The three boys were very excited, wishing their father would take them with him yet not daring to ask, for fear their stepmother should hear them and be offended.

"Fionnuala stood on the great wooden bridge which, every morning, was pushed out across the wide moat that surrounded the fort. She did not know it but her eyes filled with tears and, as she stood looking up at her father, the tears rolled down her cheeks and fell on her embroidered cloak.

"'Take me with you, father,' she said softly. Her brothers, hearing her, drew nearer and echoed her words, 'Take us with you, father!'

"He laughed, then shook his head.

"'What! Would you leave your lady mother here alone? Obey her, follow her teaching and the time before my return will pass quickly. I will bring you presents and you shall tell me all you have done and learned.'

"He sprang into his chariot, shook the reins and, as the horses leaped forward, looked back.

"Aoife was standing in the gateway of the dún with her maids and men-at-arms behind her. The children stood on the bridge, their arms stretched out to him.

"He raised his hand to his helmet in salutation to Aoife and she waved in response.

"But he could only smile at Hugh, at Fiacha and Conn. When he looked at Fionnuala, standing there pale and still, he longed to stop the horses, leap out and run back to her.

"Yet how could he? Why should he? The child would be well cared for in his absence. No harm could come to her while Aoife was in charge of the fort and all who lived within its walls.

"So he rode on, without looking back, and never again did he see his only daughter and his three sons as he saw them then."

3

An Unexpected Feast

"Go on, Gran, please!" coaxed Garry. "You can't stop there. I don't trust that stepmother."

He looked so sharply at the old lady that she bit her lip and laughed.

"Let me finish this apple," she said. "It's sweet and juicy, and my poor throat needs a bit of moistening. Besides, I'll have to think a while so that I won't leave out any important bits of the story."

"Is it tea time yet?" demanded Peter.

"Of course it isn't. We've only just had our dinner," Garry told him scornfully.

His little brother looked at him in amazement.

"We haven't had our dinner!" he declared. "I haven't! Nuala hasn't! Gran hasn't! When did you have yours?"

"Peter! You are a greedy little boy," Garry told him severely. "You ate a whole pile of sandwiches as well as two apples. You can't be hungry yet!"

"Sandwiches isn't dinner!" said Peter firmly. "They isn't, is they, Nu-nu?"

His sister frowned.

"Well, not exactly," she agreed. "But they were thick and they were nice, weren't they?"

"Want dinner," persisted Peter.

Nuala looked appealingly at her grandmother.

Mrs Brophy laughed.

"Of course, the child's right," she murmured. "He always is. I suppose I was too lazy to want to make a real dinner. But I'll tell you what I will do—I'll make a big toad-in-the-hole, with sausages and fried onions. And you can all help me. How's that?"

At once they forgot about the unfinished story. Toad-in-the-hole was a treat the way grandmother made it.

"Could we have chips too?" asked Garry, a little doubtfully.

He knew he was being greedy, but old Mrs Brophy liked giving them what they wanted. He knew that too.

"I'll cut the chips," he offered.

"I'll beat the eggs," said Nuala.

"And what will the young lads do?" asked Mrs Brophy, her eyes dancing.

The little boys looked at one another. What could they do?

"They're no use at all!" said their big brother. "They can eat and drink—that's about all. Just like Boots!"

"I know!" cried Nuala, coming to their rescue. "I'll spread the cloth and they can lay the table.

I'll tell them what to put on it. And Boots can sing to encourage us."

Danny and Peter looked at her gratefully.

She stroked the cat from between his ears right down to the tip of his tail and, knowing what was expected of him, he began to purr—long loud purrs, as if he were really singing. As she stroked, Nuala sang:

"Cats in the garden,
Cats on the wall.
Without them to sing for you
Where would you be at all?
Cats by the fireside
Purring soft and low
Cats sitting on your knee
Or following where you go."

"I don't call that noise he makes singing," said Garry scornfully. "He's no more use than the boys. And he doesn't even catch mice!"

"Poor little mice!" said Nuala. "And I'm glad he doesn't chase the birds either. I think Boots is a good, kind cat. Don't you, Gran?"

The old lady smiled.

"He's not too bad," she said. "I've known worse."

"There you are, Boots," cried Nuala. "You're being praised."

Boots shook his head, ringing the little bell which hung from the collar round his neck.

"That was Daddy's present for a good cat,"

Nuala told him.

"Hark at her," jeered Garry.

Mrs Brophy frowned at him.

"I expect it frightened the poor little mice away," scoffed Garry.

He said it so softly that Nuala didn't hear. Besides, she was following her grandmother to the kitchen.

In a moment they were all busy. Mrs Brophy put the big frying-pan on the stove, with a lump of dripping to heat. Then she pricked five sausages, one for each of them. She began to slice the onions while Garry peeled and chopped the potatoes. Soon the chips were frizzling in the pan, while a pleasant smell of fried onions filled the kitchen.

The little boys made a great fuss of laying the table. And when their grandmother put a big plate of plum cake on the table even the twins knew they were having a party.

Boots had his share—chips and some bits of sausage. Soon the only sounds, above the crackling of the fire, were the clatter of knives and forks and then the rattle of cups. They started on their second cups of tea and thick slices of cake.

"Daddy would like this," said Nuala.

Garry made a face.

"I bet he's in a grand hotel, telling jokes and stories to the other chaps," he muttered. "Gran, when will I be old enough to start off with him?"

"When you've finished with the school," Mrs Brophy told him. "'Twill be time enough then to decide what you're going to do."

Garry stopped eating. He put down the slice of cake he had been nibbling and stared at her.

"Gran, what else would I want to do but the same as Daddy?" he asked. "Just think—drive a car and be in and out of shops all day, stay in a hotel at night, have dinner when other people are just drinking tea and eating bread and butter, listen to music, make friends! Why, what else could I want to do?"

Nuala nodded. She thought it sounded a wonderful life.

But their grandmother put down her cup, clasped her hands before her on the table and looked straight at the boy.

"It's a grand life for your father," she said slowly. "But it mightn't be so good for you. He has great hopes for you, now you're doing so well at school. He was saying only the other day that if you keep on as you're going, he'd like to send you to college. But perhaps I should have let him tell you himself."

The boy flushed.

"Oh, Gran!" he whispered. "College! It sounds wonderful! And I won't let on you told me."

She smiled at him across the cluttered table.

"No need to keep it a secret," she said. "I'll let your father know I've spoken to you about it. He won't scold me."

"I shouldn't think he would!" exclaimed Garry. He laughed. "Dad scold you! He thinks the world of you, Gran! I heard him telling the schoolmaster only the other day he didn't know how he could have managed without you!"

"Can't eat any more!" sighed Peter, pushing his plate away contentedly.

"Me too," added Danny.

Mrs Brophy stood up.

"There's the crocks to be washed and the table to be cleared. Who's helping?"

"Me!" cried Nuala, running for the big tray, which stood on top of the chest of drawers against the wall.

"I'll wash up!" proclaimed Garry, who always enjoyed splashing in hot soapy water.

"I'll dry, Gran!" offered Peter, longing to be as important as the others.

"I would put everything away, only I'm not big enough to reach," reflected Danny.

"Now haven't I a houseful of great helpers," said Mrs Brophy. "I'll tell your father how good you were while he was away. And, as a reward, I'll go on with the story."

By the time they were back at the fire the world outside had changed. The wind had risen and big grey clouds were speeding across the sky. White-tipped breakers were crashing on the beach and, because the sitting-room window looked away from the village, it seemed as though they were alone in the world.

Garry built up the fire of logs and sods of turf which gave out a warm red glow. Soon they were all settled as they had been before.

"How about home lessons?" asked Mrs Brophy.

"Wouldn't it be better to finish those and have the story afterwards?"

The children laughed in chorus. Peter rubbed his head against the old woman's arm.

"Oh, Gran!" he said. "You've forgotten that tomorrow's Sunday. We did our lessons on Friday."

"'Pon me word, I had forgotten!" she declared. "With all the fuss of your father going away it slipped my mind. The moment the wind drops we must go down to the chapel and then I must go to the stores."

As a rule the children needed no coaxing to run out when they had finished a meal. But they could hear the roar of the wind and the sea outside. And they wanted to hear the rest of the story.

"When will the summer be here?" asked Nuala.

"We haven't had spring yet," Garry said.

"This is the last day of winter," Mrs Brophy told them. "If it is fine tomorrow we'll go for a long walk after Mass."

"And we'll all help with dinner when we come back," promised Nuala.

"Now for the story!" prompted Garry impatiently.

4

Four White Swans

"Where was I?" asked Mrs Brophy. "Let me see now—"

She had a big ball of blue wool on her lap, for she was making Nuala a new jumper. When she had finished that there would be three more to be made for the boys. Garry had chosen green, Danny red and Peter white.

The old woman didn't think white was the best colour for a boy who loved grubbing with his hands and wiping them on his clothes. But she thought it would be better to talk the matter over with him later, when the time came for buying the wool.

She held the crochet hook in her right hand and twisted the soft blue strand in and out the fingers of the left.

"The father had driven off in his chariot," Garry reminded her.

"Like our daddy," murmured Nuala.

Mrs Brophy nodded.

"And there were the four children left alone

with their stepmother," she began.

"Aoife tried to hide her hatred of the children and she managed to deceive the boys. But Fionnuala understood.

"'I cannot go on living with them,' thought the queen, and she determined to be rid of her stepdaughter while the father was away.

"One fine morning in spring Aoife told them she was visiting Bov the Red, where she used to live, and they were to go with her. The boys were delighted. They were tired of being shut up in the small fort, and at Bov's palace they would once again meet their cousins. But Fionnuala, without knowing why, was afraid.

"She stood watching the men as they harnessed the swift black horses to the chariot. The charioteer—an old friend of hers—came over to her.

"'Do not come on this journey, Fionnuala,' he whispered. 'Hide yourself so that you cannot be found till we have departed. You are in great danger. I will try to arrange for your safety, so that when we return you will be far away.'

"'I cannot leave my brothers without bidding them farewell,' declared the girl. 'But I will go at once and tell them.'

"'Run now!' he urged. 'You are the one in danger. Aoife does not hate the boys as she hates you. If you are away she may not harm them.'

"She was ready to obey him, for she knew he had served her mother faithfully for years. But she wanted to say goodbye to her brothers first.

"The boys came to meet her and following slowly was Aoife. Fionnuala knew she was too late.

"'Couldn't we wait till my father returns,' she pleaded. 'Suppose he comes while we are away.'

"'I will be here again in seven days,' replied Aoife. 'You need not trouble about him.'

"Fionnuala was more frightened than ever but she had to climb into the chariot.

"The morning mist lay on the fields as the horses galloped off. The boys were so excited they did not notice how still and quiet their sister sat beside them or the gloomy face of the charioteer.

"At each rise or bend of the road, Fionnuala looked back, as though she knew she would never see her home again.

"They were growing weary and had reached the Crooked Wood beside Derryvaragh when Aoife ordered the charioteer to stop.

"'Do as I bade you,' she ordered the man. 'Kill these children.'

"'This is an evil deed, Aoife,' he protested. 'I cannot do it.'

"Taking his spear from the chariot, he broke the shaft and flung away the pieces.

"'Run!' he said to Fionnuala. 'You will not be followed!'

"He knew the horses would obey no one but himself, not even Aoife, and the children were swift runners. But they clung to one another and gazed despairingly about them at the great silent lake, the towering trees and the grim, savage rocks.

"Where could they run? Fionnuala stared at the lake. Could they hide among the rushes?

"'Run!' urged the charioteer again. 'Run!'

"Taking Conn, the youngest boy, by the hands, Fionnuala ran, pulling him with her. The two other boys were quicker and reached the lake first. Plunging in among the rushes they held out their hands to their sister.

"'Keep quiet,' whispered Hugh. 'She may leave us in peace. She can't see us here.'

"'Let them go, O Queen!' pleaded the charioteer. 'They cannot harm you.'

"She let fall the spear she held for, cruel though she was, she could not kill the children by her own hand. Yet, as the charioteer gave a deep sigh of relief, she lifted the magic rod, silver and slender, which she always carried with her, and laid this spell upon them.

"'Live—but not as children!' she cried. 'From this moment you shall be creatures of air and water. The land shall no longer be your home. Children of Lir, be as swans!'

"Fionnuala felt her neck growing long and slender. Her golden hair, her clothes, changed to feathers, her arms became wings and, looking at her brothers, she saw them change into lovely white swans.

"'Why have you done this?' demanded the charioteer. 'What harm have these children ever done you? How can you be so cruel?'

"Aoife pushed him on one side and turned again to the lake.

"'This is the doom I lay upon you,' she chanted.

"*Three hundred years upon the Lake of Derryvaragh.*

Three hundred years upon the stormy Straits of Moyle.

Three hundred years where the Western ocean rolls in by Irish Glory.

"'When will this terrible enchantment end?' asked Fionnuala, her voice trembling.

"Aoife looked at her little stepdaughter and a throb of pity touched her heart.

"'When the Woman of the South shall wed the Man from the North and a clear, cold bell rings through the land, then—Nuala—the hour of your release is near,' she answered, stepping back into the chariot.

"The charioteer, with a sorrowful glance at the swans, leapt up beside her and gathered the reins in his hand. Aoife looked over her shoulder and spoke clearly:

"'This I leave you—the power of speech and the gift of song!'"

"Away thundered the horses, carrying Aoife out of sight.

"The four Swan Children huddled together.

"'Our father will find us as soon as he returns home,' said Fionnuala comfortingly. 'Or perhaps we'll wake up and discover this is only a dream.'

"On rolled the chariot, the driver urging his horses forward, for he expected that Lir, or Bov the

Red, would be able to lift the spell and the children might yet be saved.

"Aoife sat proudly, one moment delighted at her deed, the next wondering what would happen to her when it was discovered.

"Instead of returning to Lir's fort she ordered the charioteer to journey to Bov's great dún, hoping that he would protect her from Lir's wrath.

"Bov stood in the gateway, gazing at the approaching chariot and wondering that Aoife had not brought the children with her. Troubled, though he did not know why, he strode across the bridge. Before he could speak the charioteer flung down the reins and sprang to the ground.

"'Aoife has enchanted the children!' he cried. 'They are now swimming upon Derryvaragh Lake— four white swans. How can I bear that news to my master? My sorrow! If only I could have saved them!"

"Bov the Red gazed at Aoife.

"'Can this be true?' he asked her.

"Aoife gazed back without a trace of pity or of fear, yet, in her heart, she wished she had curbed her hatred.

"'It is true!' she declared. 'Lir loved his children more than me. My jealousy has grown so great I could not bear it, and they are children no longer. You cannot take off the spell. My magic is more powerful than yours.'

"Bov struggled to speak.

"'I can't help the poor unfortunate children.

But I can punish you! If Lir's dún is their home no longer, it will not be yours either.'

"He lifted his rod and spoke sternly:

"'Go forth into the wilderness of space and darkness, foul demon of the air that you have become!'

"There was a wild scream as Aoife changed from a beautiful woman into a thin, shivering waif, who was swept up into the air. She was never heard of again."

"Serve her jolly well right!" said Garry vindictively.

Mrs Brophy drew a deep breath and leaned back.

"Wisha! I'm wore out!" she murmured.

She looked around. Tears were streaming down Nuala's face, Garry was biting his lips and blinking, torn between anger and sorrow. The two little boys were squeezed together looking the picture of misery and desolation. They all felt very bad about the Children of Lir. Mrs Brophy was angry with herself.

"Now what ailed me to go telling that story," she exclaimed. "Shouldn't I have more sense! Don't I know it's one of the Three Sorrows of Story-telling? Sure, ye're too young to know all the sadness and wickedness that's in the world. It was seeing the swans made me remember the story."

She held out to Nuala the clean handkerchief she kept in the pocket of her apron.

"Wipe your eyes, pet!" she said. "And remember it all happened a long, long time ago. And happiness came to the poor Swan Children in the end."

"Honest?" asked Garry.

"Honest!" answered his grandmother firmly.

Nuala dried her eyes slowly and handed back the handkerchief.

"I wish I could keep my hankies like that," she thought. "Maybe I will when I'm grown up."

She remembered the Swan Children.

"What happened then?" she asked, her voice trembling.

"Best leave the end till tomorrow," said Mrs Brophy.

Nuala shook her head.

"I'd never go to sleep without knowing what happened!" she declared.

Garry nodded.

"Nor would I. Besides, if the ending is happy, we should know it as soon as we can."

"Mebbe you're right, lad," said his grandmother. "I'm sorry I told that story first. I don't think the other two sorrows will upset you nearly as much, perhaps not at all."

"We can wait for them till Daddy comes back," the boy told her. "Only I expect he knows the three stories."

"Mebbe," said Mrs Brophy, but her voice sounded doubtful.

"Did you tell him stories when he was a little boy?" asked Nuala curiously.

Mrs Brophy laughed.

"I did. But not that kind. He always wanted

fighting and racing and hunting stories. And, 'pon me word, he still likes them best."

"If he had been around in those days he would have stood up for the poor Swan Children, wouldn't he?" asked Nuala anxiously.

"He would indeed!" agreed the old woman.

Mrs Brophy leaned back in her chair, her hands clasped. She felt it was only fair to tell the end of the story so that Nuala could go to bed reasonably happy.

"Bov the Red sent his swiftest rider in search of Lir," she went on, "and he came at once. As the sun rose the two kings drove to Lake Derryvaragh. There they found the four Swan Children still unable to believe that they must live as birds for nine hundred years.

"When they saw Lir they swam close to the shore. He put his arms about Hugh, Fiacha and Conn and smoothed Nuala's white feathers as once he had caressed her long gleaming hair. Now her father had found them she and her brothers were sure their troubles were over.

"But, for all his power, Lir could not remove the spell Aoife had put upon them. They could speak as human beings and were clever musicians and singers. Now they sang so sweetly that, from all over Ireland, people thronged to hear them.

"Slowly they became used to their strange life and, while the Swan Children stayed on Lake Derryvaragh, great peace and kindness spread throughout the country. There were no quarrels, and each day seemed happier than the last.

"Lir camped beside the lake and, for him and the enchanted swans, those three hundred years passed like three days. He and his children belonged to the Danaans—the ancient fairy folk of Ireland—who lived far beyond mortal span.

"Bov the Red sent a proclamation throughout the land declaring that, for the sake of the Swan Children, no swans should ever again be killed in Ireland.

"The time came when Fionnuala and her brothers had to say goodbye to their own people, rise up from Derryvaragh Lake and fly to the desolate northern coast, to the Straits of Moyle, between Ireland and Alba.

"They came to Moyle in winter. Day after day a bitter wind sent the waves dashing against the Seals' Rock, the most sheltered spot they could find. The spray was frozen and the air so thick with snow they could scarcely see one another.

"Fionnuala drew her brothers under her wings, sheltering them from the bitter cold. She told them the stories she had heard in her father's dún. She taught them all she knew, so that their mind had thoughts beyond their present unhappiness. She sang the songs she had learned before Aoife put the spell upon them. Travellers, hearing her sad, lovely voice from far off, wondered if it came from sea or air. She sang:

"Wild the wind and cold the night,
Sing and dream till morning's light.

Grey the sky and fierce the sea,
Bitter is our misery.

Sorrow makes the hours long,
Suffering must follow wrong

We have done no evil deed
Lonely is the life we lead.

Sad the hours and days and years
Salt the waves and salt my tears.

Shall I ever hear that bell
Cruel Aoife did foretell?

Cold and sweet and silver clear
Filled with comfort, not with fear.

Sad my dreams and sad my song,
Hours and days and years are long.

"'If we went on shore,' said Conn, 'we could find shelter.'

"Fionnuala shook her head.

"'We cannot go on shore until our doom comes to an end.'

"'Then we won't always be like this?' he asked eagerly.

"'Not always!'"

The four Brophy children, listening to their grandmother, sighed with relief.

"I am glad," said Nuala. "Now I know the Swan Children's troubles won't go on for ever, I think I can bear the rest."

Mrs Brophy smiled at her.

"The next story I tell will have laughter in it from beginning to end," she decided.

"Please go on, Gran!" coaxed Garry.

"First put a log on the fire," the old woman told him. "The wind is rising and I feel the cold."

The others sat silent till Garry came back, carrying two big logs. He put one on top of the glowing fire and laid the other just inside the fender. Quickly he went back to his stool against the hearth and looked up eagerly.

"Now, Gran!" he said.

5

The Saddest Story

Mrs Brophy sighed but went on at once.

"Even summer was harsh in that northern region. The Swan Children were lonelier than ever because now their own people could not come to them and there were no dwellings along that rocky coast. Fishing boats from Alba kept farther to the north and only wandering birds came near. They sang of strange lands where even the night was hot and great forests spread over plains and climbed mountains, where rivers seemed as mighty as the sea.

"'There are birds, even more wonderful then you, in those far countries,' they told the Swan Children. 'Some glow like jewels, others dwell on mountain tops and fly so high they are lost in the clouds. We have heard birds singing so melodiously that we longed to stay and listen for ever. But never have we heard such singing as yours!'

"Seabirds nested on the cliffs and the Swan Children watched them building homes, bringing up their young ones, darting through the air, swooping, fishing, swimming, quarrelling. But these were not friendly. They pretended not to see the large white birds who spoke like human beings and sang so sadly.

"Yet the Children of Lir found happiness in swimming and flying, but more still in their affection for one another and in talking of what would become of them when their time of enchantment was over.

"At last that three hundred years came to an end, but they were no older than when they had driven with Aoife to Lake Derryvaragh. Sometimes they thought they had been swans for only a short while, and once Hugh, the eldest boy, dreamed his father came to take him home. But he woke as he was stepping into the chariot.

"Next day the worst storm they had known raged along the Straits of Moyle. The waves rose so high against the cliffs the swans were separated. Fionnuala saw her brothers beaten under the sea. She called them but the screaming wind prevented them hearing her voice as she was swept away.

"'If only I can find them,' she thought, 'I'll never complain again whatever happens!'

"That's just the way I'd feel," Nuala told herself, looking round at her brothers.

Gran Brophy went on in a soft, clear voice.

"At dawn, bruised and weary, their wings tattered, the four swans found one another. First to Seals' Rock came Fionnuala, then Hugh, flying down the wind and, a little while after, Conn and Fiacha.

"'We are going west,' Fionnuala told them. 'I think we will never suffer so much again.'

"They flew across Ireland by night. When they saw, far below, the flickering light of torches, the Swan Children wondered if ever they would live within walls and know the happiness of being with friends in their own home.

"They came down near Erris Point in north-west Mayo. There, among the bird islands, they entered upon the last three hundred years of their doom.

"Fionnuala and her brothers felt very lonely, and one winter the sea from Erris to Aran was frozen over so that they could not swim. A young farmer, whose name was Erric, heard them singing in the distance. Going out in the early morning he searched and searched—led by the sound—until he discovered the enchanted swans huddled on the rocks. He became their friend and learned their story. Each day he came to talk with them.

"'It is time we went to look on our father's dún again,' Fionnuala told her brothers.

"Joyfully they rose into the cold grey air and flew over the frozen land, Fionnuala leading, Hugh close beside her and the younger brothers following behind.

"'It should be here!' declared Fionnuala suddenly. 'There are no halls or buildings of any kind, nor any people. Our father's home cannot be here,' said Hugh.

"The others joined them and, circling round,

they tried to discover some trace of Lir's old home.

"All they could see were a few grass-grown mounds inside a dry trench, topped by withered bushes and patches of nettles.

"'It cannot be here!' cried Fiacha.

"'It is here!' his sister told him. 'It was!'

"Now she realised their past was gone from them for ever. They would never see their own people again in the home they had known.

"This was the most unhappy day of their lives. Sad and bewildered they returned to the wild western shore where they had made their home, and saw Erric wandering along the frozen strand, searching anxiously for them.

"'I feared you might never come back,' he said.

"'We went to seek our father's fort,' Fionnuala told him. 'But the doom that is on us has hidden everything we once knew.'

"Suddenly the thin sound of a bell rang through the still air. Startled, the three brothers drew together. But Fionnuala remembered.

"'It is the bell whose ringing foretells our release,' she said. 'And yet I am afraid!'

"'Do not be afraid!' said Erric. 'Yonder dwells one who understands these mysteries. Wait here for me. I will bring him to you.'

"He hurried away but soon returned, and with him came the hermit, Kermec, who had built his cell and chapel on one of the rocky inlets. His long white robe, his noble face and friendly eyes comforted Fionnuala.

"'Here is another friend we have found,' she thought.

"'Peace be with you, Children of Lir!' he called.

"'Peace!' echoed the swans.

"They swam in close to the shore, while the hermit seated himself on a rock and they looked at him in silence.

"'Long ago I heard of the singing swans,' said the old man. 'I prayed that I might come to know them. Tell me your history!'

"'We were four happy children,' began Fionnuala. The old man and his young companion did not move or speak as the swans recalled the joys of their early days and all the misery that followed. Erric hid his face and wept, but the hermit seemed held in a dream.

"Fionnuala's head drooped with weariness as she finished.

"'Aoife was cruel,' said the hermit gently. 'She drove you from the Land of Youth and closed its gates against you. But God has spared you for a greater destiny.'

"Day by day he taught Fionnuala and her brothers the Christian faith and told how Ireland had changed with the coming of the Milesians and of St Patrick's teaching. Slowly the long sad years slipped from their minds. They sang for Erric and the old hermit as once they sang for the Danaans, in pagan times, only more enchantingly than ever.

"Others heard their singing and crowds gathered on the Mayo coast, hoping to catch a glimpse of the swans. But they hid from everyone except their two friends.

"The fame of the Children of Lir reached the Princess Deoca of Munster, who was betrothed to a Connacht chief named Lairgren. He longed to give Deoca everything she could wish. But she asked only one wedding gift—the four singing swans. The hermit would not give them up and Erric strove to protect them. But the Connacht men were strong and determined. They bound the Children of Lir with golden chains and dragged them off to Deoca.

"Erric and the hermit followed all the way to the Court of Munster.

"As the swans were brought before the princess their white feathers dropped away. Instead of graceful white birds or the lovely Danaan children, the horrified Deoca saw four withered creatures incredibly old.

"Lairgren, appalled at what he had done, rushed from the court while Erric and the hermit knelt beside Fionnuala and her brothers.

"'Lay us in one grave,' she said. 'Conn at my right hand and Fiacha at my left. But put Hugh before me, for that was the way I sheltered them on those bitter winter nights upon the Straits of Moyle.'

"The hermit baptised them as they died. He and Erric obeyed Fionnuala's wishes and laid the four in the one grave. So they went to heaven. But the young farmer and the old hermit remembered the

the Swan Children to the end of their days.

As their grandmother reached the finish of her story the fire, which had burned with a red glow, had fallen in and only a small heap of grey turf ash remained. They were so interested in the story they had not noticed the dwindling fire. Now the old woman hugged her shawl about her.

"Hurry to bed, children!" she said. "Don't feel too sad about the four Swan Children. Remember—they had one another and they came to real happiness in the end."

6

A Long Letter

By Monday morning it seemed to the children that their father had been away for weeks and weeks. The sun was hidden by banks of grey cloud, the breakers came roaring in, crashing on the beach, tossing torrents of spray over the sea wall. Waves were leaping up at the cliffs.

Windows dripped sadly, smoke blew down the chimney into the room. When Gran Brophy opened the door and came in from the kitchen even Garry, who loved school, was hoping she would say they must stay home and miss lessons. But she didn't.

"Put on your tammies, coats and mufflers," she said. "It's time you were on your way to school. I know it's a bit early but you may meet Dan the Post. If he has a letter for me will you run back with it, just in case it's from your father, though I'm not expecting one yet?"

"Of course I will," promised Garry.

"Can we bring home anything from the stores?" asked Nuala. "Then you needn't go out. We could take the basket and leave it in the cloakroom."

Her grandmother smiled.

"Thank you, dear. But it will do me good to have a breath of fresh air. Did the wind keep you young ones awake?"

Garry shook his head.

"Nothing keeps me awake!" he declared proudly. "When I go to bed and shut my eyes—I'm asleep!"

Nuala frowned.

"I did sleep. But I think I dreamed all the time about the Swan Children. It was a strange dream."

"You must go to bed earlier tonight," Mrs Brophy told her. "I kept you up too long telling that story. I should have remembered the time."

"You'll tell us another story tonight, won't you, Gran?" coaxed Garry. "Maybe you could think of one that would make us laugh!"

"Maybe," agreed the old woman.

As they went out the three of them had to hold the door so that the wind wouldn't blow it wide open, for it was growing fiercer every minute.

"Hold hands," said their grandmother, "and keep your heads down. Let Garry and Nuala keep in front—that will shelter the little ones. If you do meet Dan the Post there is no need for anyone but Garry to come back. The wind is too wild for the younger ones to be running backwards and forwards. Goodbye now and learn all you can!"

She shut the door after them and stood at the window watching the four struggling against the storm.

"'Tis well we're not far from the village," she

murmured. "It's desperate weather. Look at those poor swans tossing like seaweed in the waves. Thanks be, Tim will be snug in his motor-car. I wonder what secret he's keeping from me. Ah well, he won't keep it long. I know me boy Tim!"

She filled the kettle and set it on the fire, gathered the breakfast crocks and piled them in the big green enamel bowl. While waiting for the kettle to boil she considered what special dish she should make for dinner.

"The children will need a bit of comfort when they do get back," she told herself. "What's wrong with a boiled meat dumpling? Only there's not a scrap of meat in the house. I'd best go down to the village at once in case Ben Kelleher is sold out. And the kettle will be safer on the hearth till I return."

Boots, from the shelter of the low-growing elder bush by the gate, watched Gran Brophy as she went by without seeing him.

Snugly wrapped in a thick shawl draped over her head, and reaching almost to her ankles, she set out for the village, the big market bag swinging on her arm.

"I'd as well bring home all I can," she thought. "The storm may last and I won't want too much of it."

Taking advantage of every bit of shelter provided by walls, rocks and trees, she made her way along the path until it joined the shore road. There she stopped to catch her breath.

"I should have let the children take care of the messages," she said regretfully. "They enjoy the importance of going to the stores. But, sure, how could a child like Nuala know what to choose, and I hadn't time to make a list. I'd best stir me stumps. The sooner I get the job done the sooner I'll be back in shelter."

To her dismay the sea was washing over the shore road.

"I wonder did Garry have the sense to take the back way?" she reflected. "He's a sensible boy— sometimes—and maybe he did. Now which way would Dan the Post come? I shouldn't have bothered Garry to look out for him when I was coming to the village myself."

The back way was sheltered by low-growing trees peeping over the garden walls of the bigger houses on the sea road. Mrs Brophy was able to walk more quickly at the back of the houses, but she was thankful when she came to the square where the shops, clustered on four sides, gave more protection from the wind. She was crossing to the butcher's shop when a voice from the post office hailed her.

"Hi, Mrs Brophy! I've a letter for ye! If I'm not mistaken, 'tis from Himself. Isn't he the great lad! He never forgets! He only went on Saturday, didn't he?"

The old woman nodded.

"You're right there, Dan!" she said as she took the letter he handed her with some surprise, for it was far bulkier than Tim's usual letters.

Dan nodded with understanding.

"'Tisn't often he writes that much," he said. "I've known when ye were lucky to get a postcard in a fortnight. This was posted in Sligo. That's why you've had it so soon!"

Mrs Brophy did not answer. She had a sudden longing to go back as quickly as she could to discover what had happened that her son should write at such length.

"It might be a bit he'd read in the paper and thought ye might miss it," Dan remarked, his head on one side, his eyes fixed on the letter. "Still, it might be important. Wouldn't it be as well to step inside the post office and read it there?"

She shook her head.

"I'll wait till I get home!"

Dan sighed.

"Isn't it queer now! I carry all the letters for this place, yet there's never one for me. Sometimes I feel I'll be driven to write one to meself!"

"Wait till I get away from here," chuckled one of the men lounging in the doorway. "The minit I'm broke, I'll write you for the loan of ten bob. That should please ye."

Dan the Post shrugged his shouldered and went back to the office. Mrs Brophy turned to the butcher's shop. Next she went to the stores. Instead of filling her bag, she asked the store-keeper to send her order.

"'Twill be a bit heavy," she said. "Besides, the

wind is so high I'll have enough trouble carrying myself."

The store-keeper laughed.

"You're lucky you haven't my weight to carry around. But don't worry! The boy is just going out with the messages. He'll bring yours and he won't be long after you."

"Thank you kindly!" the old woman remarked.

A man standing by the counter turned to her.

"If you've finished with the shops," he said, "I'll give you a lift home. 'Twill only take a few minutes and you'd be blown off your feet if you try to manage it alone."

"You're very good," murmured Mrs Brophy. "Amn't I the lucky woman! Me messages are being sent and I'll be riding home like a lady!"

The friendly man helped Mrs Brophy into his car. "Many a time your lad's given me a lift before I bought this old yoke. I'm only too glad to do a turn for a Brophy."

She smiled her thanks and settled back comfortably. The noise of wind and waves was deadened for a moment. It seemed no time at all when he pulled up at her home and said cheerfully: "Well, here we are!"

He helped her out, and before she had opened the door of the house he had started up the car and was off.

"Now for the letter!" she said aloud. "What in the world has made Tim write this great bundle and so soon after leaving home? 'Pon me word! He must have written it before he went. Now isn't that very queer?"

She put the unopened letter on the table, made a pot of tea, put milk and sugar in the cup, poured in the tea then took up the letter. Still she did not open the envelope, but began to sip the hot, strong, sweet tea.

It was even more comforting than usual.

"Why do I need comforting?" she asked herself. "Amn't I the queer old one?"

At last she tore the top of the envelope and pulled out the bundle of sheets. Each piece of paper was filled on both sides with his neat, small writing.

She read slowly. Before she had reached the end of the first page her eyes opened wide. She frowned, shook her head, sighed and, when she reached the end, she sat very still.

"I wonder," she said softly. "I wonder."

She read the whole letter through again, from the first page to the last, each one more slowly than the one before.

"The dear lad!" she said. "But whatever ailed me to tell the children that sad story about the Swan Children and their wicked stepmother? Here he is bringing home a stepmother to them and I had to tell them a story of one of the worst stepmothers in history! 'Tisn't fair to them, tisn't fair to me only son either, who thinks he's doing a fine thing for them—mebbe he is! And 'tisn't fair to the girl that's coming into this house. Ah, what can I do to prevent my story-telling from making mischief? What can I do?"

She sat staring into the fire, shaking her head and puzzling over the problem.

"If only I'd chosen any other story," she thought regretfully.

A thump on the door roused her. She jumped up and ran to open it. Andy Murphy, the boy from the stores, stood there with a loaded basket. His bicycle leaned against the garden wall.

"Come in! Come in out of the wind!" she cried. He came in with Boots trotting eagerly after him.

"The poor baste was being blown along the path," chuckled the messenger boy, his hair tousled by the wind. "But he's that proud he wouldn't let me carry him! It'll take me four times as long to get back. I free-wheeled all the way here but I'll have to push every inch going home."

He followed Mrs Brophy into the warm, comfortable room and leaned against the table while she unpacked the basket.

"It was good of Mr Kelleher to send all my shopping. But it will be a hard job for you going back. Would you like a cup of hot tea to help you on the road? The pot is keeping warm by the fire."

"If you're asking me what I'd really like," said the boy, "I'd sooner have a cup of your elderberry wine. My mother says you are nearly as famous for that as you are for story-telling."

Mrs Brophy laughed.

"We'll have a sup each. It's a cheerful drink for

a cold day, for it does keep out the cold. I have some in the saucepan ready to give the children when they come from school. I hate to think of them in that terrible wind."

"The master says it will be changing before the morning school is over," said Andy consolingly. "And they may be blown home!"

He stood there sipping his elderberry wine and gazing round the room.

"Wish we had nice pictures on our walls at home," he said. "Now I must get back. Mr Kelleher told me not to stay talking, wasting your time and his time, as well as my own. Thank you for the drink, it was grand."

Mrs Brophy closed the door after him and went back to her son's letter.

"It's the longest I ever remember him writing," she told the big black cat, who was stretched on the rug before the fire, purring with great satisfaction. "Oh dear, how can I tell the children what's going to happen?"

She looked very perplexed as she turned the pages slowly.

"So he's bringing home a young wife. I'm glad he's told the girl what's before her. To bring up four children is not easy. She must be good and kind to take it on. I do hope we will be friends! I always longed for a daughter and this may be the answer to my prayer. If only I hadn't told that awful story! I might have told them about Cuchulain or Queen Maeve. Or I could have told

them about the Good People who play their tricks.
That wouldn't have made any mischief."

She poured out another glass of the rich, purple
wine. Boots begged for some but, when she let him
sniff, he turned away in disgust.

"Wait till you smell your dinner," she laughed;
"there'll be plenty for you then."

Boots listened, rolled on his back, yawned,
tucked in his white paws and slept.

The fire was red and not a wisp of smoke came
down the chimney, for the wind was changing its
course. The raindrops still tapped urgently at the
windows and streamed down the panes.

The old woman scrubbed large potatoes and put
them in a baking tin. She took a big white
cauliflower that had come from the garden and
prepared it for dinner.

"I hope the girl that comes will be happy," she
mused, her thoughts returning to the stranger her
son was bringing home. I like her name—Eva
O'Mahony. And she will be Eva Brophy. I like the
sound of that too. And she comes from Cork City.
They're friendly, easy-going people in those parts.
Tim says she has a lovely voice and will be able
to sing at the Sunday concerts. He says she knows
all the new songs and is longing to learn the old
ones from me. I must tell the children at once.
Now why did he never mention her before? Perhaps
he wanted to make sure first.

"Maybe I shouldn't have talked so much to the
children about their own mother. I couldn't bear

they should forget her. How hard it is to know the best thing to do. I must tell them when they're feeling lazy and content after dinner. I'll try to make it seem like another story. But why, oh why, did I ever tell them about the Children of Lir!"

7

That Wasn't a Story

Before the morning school was over the wind died down, but rain was falling steadily. The children had their hooded macs, but Garry thought it babyish to pull his hood over his head or to avoid puddles. He splashed along, swinging his arms, humming loudly, though he secretly envied his sister who dodged the puddles and had her chin buried inside the collar of her mac, with her hands deep in the pockets. Danny imitated his brother. Peter copied Nuala.

Their grandmother saw them coming and had the door open, ready for them.

"In with you and off with those wet macs! Garry, you hang them on the kitchen door. Change your boots. Here are your slippers, warm and snug. I'm glad two of you had the sense to keep as dry as you could. Danny is only a silly little boy—but you, Garry, should have more sense. Still, you're in now. I'm glad you haven't to go back this afternoon. Half-holidays are some use when the weather's this way."

"I don't mind the weather," said Garry scornfully.

"Gran, did you get the letter from Daddy?" asked Nuala.

Mrs Brophy did not answer. She went out to the kitchen and lifted the lid from the big saucepan to gain time, for she was troubled.

"She didn't hear you," Garry told his sister.

Nuala knew her grandmother had heard her, for she had seen the old woman's sudden start. She knew that Gran Brophy wasn't easily troubled. What could be wrong now?

"Garry, you help me bring in the pudding and the vegetables. And you, Nuala, pour out the hot drink!" said Mrs Brophy over her shoulder.

"Didn't you get a letter from Daddy?" persisted Nuala.

Garry saw his grandmother bite her lip and shake her head. He guessed she was worried and frowned at his sister, warningly. She nodded and, to Mrs Brophy's relief, there were no more questions.

"You said you'd let me take out the pudding," Garry told her reproachfully as she untied the steaming cloth.

"I'm sorry—I forgot," she said. "But isn't it grand to have it all hot, and you children tired and battered, struggling with the weather."

They both laughed. The smaller boys settled down comfortably to their dinner. It wasn't until the dinner was finished, and they were all sitting round the fire with cups of tea and chunks of hot apple cake, that Nuala spoke again.

"Won't you tell us now, Gran?" she asked. "I mean—isn't there a letter?"

Mrs Brophy leaned back in her chair, nodded and closed her eyes.

"I know!" exclaimed Garry in sudden alarm. "Dad's going to America! He didn't want to tell us. But he is coming back, isn't he? He wouldn't go away and leave us, would he? Not Dad!"

Mrs Brophy laughed, opened her eyes and sat up straight.

"No, no, child!" she exclaimed. "Whatever put such an idea into your head?"

"The Nolans' father went, and Mr O'Keeffe too, only last month," said the boy. "I thought perhaps Dad had to go, and you couldn't bear to tell us. If it isn't that, it can't be so bad, can it?"

His grandmother looked at him almost gratefully.

"You are a sensible boy!" she said. "No, it's nothing so bad. Indeed, it's not bad at all! Your father is bringing home a new mother and I thought it might seem queer to have a stranger in the house. But he says she's a dear, kind girl who loves children and will do her best to make you all happy."

Now that the news was told, Mrs Brophy felt quite different. The newcomer might, indeed, be someone they would all love.

"What a foolish woman I am," she thought. "Such things happen every day, all over the world.

And usually they make for happiness. If only I hadn't told the children that Swan Legend!"

Nuala looked at her solemnly.

"We're to have a stepmother?" she asked slowly.

Her voice did not rise above a whisper.

Her grandmother nodded.

"It could be grand news," she said. "Besides, you must think of your father!"

Nuala sighed and leaned forward.

"You know what you told us," she said, even more softly than before, "about the Children of Lir. Was it a true story?"

The old woman considered this.

"That wasn't a story. That was a legend," she explained. "If anything like that *did* happen, it was long, long agō. No one has such power now. We live in different times. Besides, don't you trust your father? Don't you know he would never bring home anyone who wouldn't be kind to you? You can't believe that, Nuala!"

Nuala sat up very straight. Her hands were clasped round her knees, but they were trembling. So was her voice when she spoke.

"When King Lir brought that wicked, cruel woman home, he thought she was good and kind. Yet look what she did!"

Gran Brophy gazed at Nuala with troubled eyes. She had never seen her granddaughter so determined, yet so frightened.

"I'll make very sure what kind of legend I tell them next time," she thought. "Oh, why did I do it? Why?"

"I'm thirsty!" exclaimed Peter suddenly. "Can't we have some more nice hot drink? Just a drop, Grannie!"

Boots stood on his hind legs, waved his front paws and miaowed.

"Ah, the creature!" said Mrs Brophy. "He wants to be made a fuss of. Let him sit on the sofa between the two of you!"

Nuala sat staring out of the window, and her grandmother, without turning, knew she was looking at the four white swans.

Garry, as he shifted to make room for the cat, turned and looked too.

"You know, Gran, it is queer—those swans out there—just when you told us about the swans in the legend. I've never seen four swans together like that. One, two or a dozen! Never four!"

His grandmother had just come in from the kitchen, carrying the jug of hot drink. As she passed behind the sofa she bent over the boy.

"Ye young eejit!" she muttered. "Haven't ye a haporth of sense? Can't you see it upsetting your sister?"

Garry started, looked at Nuala and understood.

"I am an eejit!" he thought. "Of course Nuala is mixing those swans up with the ones in the legend."

He swallowed his hot drink in such a hurry that he began to cough, and kept on so long they were all alarmed, all except Danny, who was talking to the cat, as no one else would listen to his account of what happened in school that morning.

"Teacher put that silly Jimmy Nolan in the cupboard, and he's got to stay there till he knows his six times six," he announced.

Boots yawned. He had no interest in school happenings.

"Then he'll be there till next week," declared Garry scornfully. "And she ought to put you with him!"

Mrs Brophy nearly dropped the best jug she was holding.

"Do you mean to say that nice Miss Florrie shut that poor little fellow in the cupboard?" she cried. "I can't believe it!"

Nuala smiled.

"Oh no!" she explained. "Miss Florrie only pretended. When he said he'd try his hardest, she let him off! She did, Gran!"

"Dear, dear!" said Mrs Brophy to herself. "I should have had more sense. I'm nearly as bad as Nuala! Times have changed and people are not so cruel. I must try to make Nuala understand."

The hot apple cake had made them all feel more cheerful. Without being asked, Garry started on the washing-up. Nuala did the drying and the little boys polished the knives, forks and spoons.

"Now aren't you good children!" exclaimed Mrs Brophy. "That young woman who's coming doesn't know what a good house she's coming into, though I expect your father has told her all about it."

"When will she be coming?" asked Garry.

"Next Wednesday morning," Mrs Brophy told him.

"Only three days," thought Nuala sorrowfully.

"Not much time to get the children used to the notion," said the grandmother to herself.

But she knew the only one she need trouble about was Nuala. Already the boys were getting excited at the coming of the stranger.

Mrs Brophy had a feeling of excitement too. She had always longed for a daughter. The children's mother and herself had been great friends and she often felt lonely without her.

As she pondered over the future she picked up her knitting.

"Let me see how much you've grown," she said, drawing Peter close to her and measuring the material against him.

"That's not my pullover!" cried Peter. "Mine's white!"

"A white pullover would look foolish in this weather," she told him, "and you would soon make it grubby."

"Want white!" he said firmly.

"All the other boys will call you cissy," chuckled Danny. "Cissy in his white gown!"

The little fellow looked doubtful. He had a great respect for Danny's opinion.

"He can have my old white pullover, can't he, Gran?" offered Nuala. "It's got smaller and I've got bigger. I'd love the green pullover you were going to make for him."

"A good idea," agreed Mrs Brophy. "I'll make it into a jumper with a turned-down collar for you."

Peter opened his mouth to roar.

"What do you want now?" asked his grandmother.

She spoke more sharply than usual. She was feeling anxious. Nuala's sad face troubled her and she wanted the newcomer to receive a warm welcome. Peter looked at her in shocked surprise.

"Don't you love me any more?" he asked hopefully. "I'll wear a green jumper if you want me to. Honest I will, Gran."

"Ah, the dote!" she chuckled, and hugged him. "You see, the white jumper would get dirty so quickly."

He nodded.

"Can I have a ginger biscuit to make up?" he coaxed.

"That fella never loses a chance," said Garry scornfully.

Yet he was pleased, too, to be nibbling the hard, brown, gingery biscuit, for their grandmother gave them one each.

"What about that poem you were learning during the week, Garry—the long one?" she asked. "Could you say it? Then Nuala can sing the song she's practising for the *Feis Cheoil*."

"A concert!" cried Garry with enthusiasm.

Garry was delighted to say the longest poem he had learned—"The Battle of Fontenoy." Nuala sang

"Dear Harp of My Country" while Danny and Peter struggled through "Out and Make Way for the Bold Fenian Men." The others helped them and, by the time they had finished, they all felt a great deal more cheerful.

"Isn't it queer," thought the grandmother. "When the heart is low there's nothing like a good rousing song for cheering a body up."

Even Nuala had almost forgotten what had been troubling her, and when Mrs Brophy asked her to sing "The Castle of Dromore" she started at once and sang it sweetly. They all joined in with her.

Nothing would satisfy Danny and Peter but to sing an old ballad called "Paddy Hegarty's Old Leather Britches."

"I don't like that at all," declared Mrs Brophy. "It's terrible vulgar. I don't know where they learn such things. Miss Florrie doesn't teach them that king of song, I'm sure."

"They learned it off old Séamus Rafferty," Garry told her. "People give him money for singing it. He told me he gets twice as much for singing that than he gets for 'The Irish Widow's Message to Her Son in America.'"

"That's sad," explained Nuala. "Nobody likes being made sad. It's all about a mother that will never see her son any more because he emigrated to America. But it's not true now, is it? I mean nowadays people can go there and back so quickly, they don't feel miserable when they go away."

"When I'm grown up I'll go to America," Garry bragged.

"I'll go to Egypt and climb on top of the pyramids," said Nuala.

Her brother looked at her in wonder.

"But Egypt's geography," he scoffed. "It's like going into an atlas."

Nuala looked at her grandmother.

"Isn't it better to go to a real strange place if you do go away from home?" she asked. "By this time America must be nearly full up with people from Ireland. Soon there won't be enough room for the people who belong there."

"Who does belong there?" asked Danny.

"Red Indians," Garry told him, making a fierce grimace.

"Red!" exclaimed the little boy. "Real red? Red all over?"

Mrs Brophy laughed.

"Don't be telling the child such nonsense," she said. "The Red Indians were there first. They weren't really red, only dark. But they painted themselves when they went out fighting, the way other people wear bright uniforms. They lived in tents, but they called them wigwams. There weren't so many of them and America is a big place, so those who hadn't room in their own countries went swarming in there."

By this time they were all comfortable and drowsy by the fire. Their grandmother gave them hot soup and toast for supper. Garry had almost forgotten the news about his father. But Nuala remembered and, looking at her pale, determined face, Mrs Brophy knew that she was still troubled.

"The poor child! What can I do or say to comfort her?" she asked herself.

8

Running Away

Nuala had her own little room, one of the two attics at the top of the house. Her father had covered the walls with coloured wallpaper telling the story of Snow White and the Seven Dwarfs. Her grandmother had hung flowered muslin curtains to the small window and had draped a patchwork counterpane on the bed. She thought the room was the prettiest she had ever seen.

She had a set of shelves for her books, a wooden chest for her clothes and four holy pictures on the walls, one each side of the door and one each side of the window.

"No wonder she has good dreams," reflected Mrs Brophy.

She thought too it was not surprising that Nuala never grumbled when it was time to go to bed.

Yet this night when the boys were yawning and saying good night to their grandmother, Nuala still sat by the fire, her head in her hands, her eyes watching the flickering flames.

"Isn't it a pity we can't have chestnuts," complained Garry. "That fire would be just right for roasting them."

"What's wrong with roast praties?" asked his grandmother. "I've a few good-sized ones. They take a while to roast, so remind me tomorrow evening and we'll have them for supper. Now, Nuala, don't let the boys be first upstairs. I count on you to set a good example."

At last the children were all away and, as Mrs Brophy turned out the lamp in the big room and went slowly upstairs to bed, she told herself that when their father came home he would know how to comfort Nuala and everything would be all right.

"She's such a kind child," she said to herself, "and I'm sure she'll get on well with her new mother."

She paused with her hand on the door of her own room wondering if she should climb to the attic and have her usual bedtime talk with Nuala. But she was tired and felt a little puzzled herself as to what difference the change would make in all their lives.

"Mebbe I'd better leave her father to do the talking," she thought. "Nuala and the girl who's coming in might take a liking to each other straight off. If I go explaining and coaxing, it may worry the child more than ever. When the new teacher came to the school, Nuala and the others were all a bit upset. But in a couple of days Nuala was saying what a darling she was. It could be that way now. I'll not disturb her."

In her little attic Nuala stood by the window staring out into the night. She heard the boys laughing and talking. She heard her grandmother's footsteps on the stairs and half hoped, half feared she would come in to her.

The door below closed; the boys were silent and the only sounds were the wind from the mountains and the beating of the waves on the shore.

Her clear eyes could see the rocky inlets in the bay and four white swans drifting on the tossing sea.

"Gran might have come up," she thought resentfully. "Still, I couldn't tell her what I feel. She wouldn't understand. She always likes people— always. She doesn't ever believe they can really be horrid, even when she knows they are."

The wind swept past the house, whistling and sighing. The moon made a silver path across the waves.

"I wish Uncle Des and Aunt Maureen lived in Craigcullen instead of at Castle Moat. They'd stand up for us. If only they knew," she said aloud.

The longer Nuala thought over her troubles the more she felt they would be settled if only her uncle and aunt knew about them before her father came home with the stranger.

"If I went to them," she mused, "I'm sure it wouldn't be so bad. They would tell me what to do and I wouldn't be alone."

Usually every few months her aunt and uncle came to stay at the house in Craigcullen, and often Tim Brophy drove his family over to Castle Moat. The distance was not great, but it was nearly an hour's drive the way they went by the lake, for it was a winding road. He said he could walk there in half the time by keeping along the coast. The bog road was shorter too, but he would never take it.

"If Garry would come with me we could tell Uncle Des and Aunt Maureen all about it," Nuala said to herself. "Then we'd have nothing to worry about!"

Suddenly she made up her mind.

"I can't tell Gran! She wouldn't let me go! I must go at once while she's asleep. I'll put on my thick shoes and my warm new coat and start straight away."

Nuala was never afraid of the dark, but she hated loneliness. If only Garry would come too!

But she daren't try to wake him. Often he slept so soundly he had to be shaken and shaken when it was time to get up. She must go alone. It would be no use to rouse the younger lads. They'd never understand!

The outdoor shoes, coats and mufflers were kept in a press by the side of the little square hall near the front door. Nuala stepped noiselessly from her room and tiptoed down the stairs.

She reached the kitchen and found the door closed. So also was the door of the big living-room.

Boots was there, curled up in the armchair. Nuala saw his green eyes shining in the darkness, not far from the still glowing fire.

"Miaow!" he said in greeting.

"Sh!" Nuala warned him.

For the first time she wished he was a dog. Then he could go with her. But Boots was too fond of his home to go far away.

"If only Garry was coming with me," thought Nuala.

As she looked about her Nuala heard a creak on the stairs. Could it be her grandmother?

She crouched behind the big chair and held her breath. The door, which she had left ajar, was pushed open and she could see a shadowy figure standing there, looking straight at her.

"Who's there?" came a cautious whisper.

Nuala smiled in relief. It was Garry.

"It's me," she whispered.

"Did you come down for a drink?" he asked softly. "I'm thirsty too."

"No, I'm running away," she answered boldly.

"Running away!" he echoed incredulously. "You! Running away!" Almost under his breath, he added: "Where to? What for?"

Nuala felt cross. Surely he didn't need to be told.

"To Aunt Maureen and Uncle Desmond," she told him.

Her voice was quite sharp and he held up a finger in warning.

"Don't wake everyone, you noodle! What are you running away for? Wait, I'll light the lamp then we can see what we're up to."

She did not answer. She saw his shadowy head nodding. He understood! Of course he did!

"I suppose it's because of the stepmother," he sighed. "But what can they do? They'd never interfere."

"They'd stand by us," she answered. "They might let us live with them."

He stood considering this, then he felt on the mantelpiece for the box of matches and lit the lamp.

"They couldn't do that without Dad agreeing," he said at last. "And they'd never go against Gran. She wouldn't want you to leave home. And what about Dad?"

"You needn't come if you don't want to," Nuala told him scornfully. "I can go by myself!"

"As if I'd let you!" he whispered. "You'd get lost—you don't know the way. Remember, I've walked there with Dad—you haven't! I'll put on my thick shoes and coat. Then we'll set off. Bring some food in case it takes longer than we think. But I don't like leaving Gran!"

Nuala had been feeling desperate and frightened. Now she began to be excited. She made her way to where Mrs Brophy's shopping-bag hung on a nail at the side of the food cupboard. Lifting it down she filled the bag carefully.

Moonlight flooded the small kitchen, so she

had no difficulty in finding the biscuit tin. She took out several handfuls. Next she packed in a piece of cheese and a box of dates, then she crammed in a lump of seed-cake.

"Ready?" whispered Garry urgently, tiptoeing up to her.

She nodded.

They moved towards the front door. Suddenly the boy clutched his sister's arm.

"What's that?" he asked. "If it isn't those blessed kids!"

Nuala looked up. On the stairs outside the boys' room the two little figures were standing together, dressed in their night clothes. Each carried a bundle, the day clothes they had taken off before going to bed.

"Go back to bed!" Garry hissed. "You'll wake Grannie. We're just going for a bit of a walk."

"We're coming too!" declared Danny.

Luckily he spoke softly, but his voice was very determined.

"Be good boys," coaxed Nuala. "You don't want to wake poor Grannie. She's very tired!"

"You're running away!" Peter told her. "We're coming!"

"Silly little eejits!" said their big brother scornfully. "Why on earth should we run away?"

"'Cause you're dreadful frightened of the stepmother!" Danny said. "So's us! Didn't Gran tell us all about it!"

"Bother!" muttered Garry. "We can't take them!

We'll have to give in! Go back to bed, you two! We'll be up soon!"

"No!" said Nuala. "We must take them—it's only fair. Come in to the fire and put on your clothes—I'll help you. Garry, please get their boots."

While Nuala buttoned their coats, tied their bootlaces and tried not to wish that they would say they were sleepy and wanted to go back to bed, Garry went round the kitchen pretending they were going to camp on a desert island and trying to remember all they would need.

His school satchel was packed tight, so was Nuala's, as well as the shopping-bag. But now there were four of them instead of two, and that would mean more provisions.

"Ah well," he told himself, "we may get there before long."

He shook his head.

"We might if it was only Nuala and me! But these two will spoil everything. And Gran will be worried to death."

At last they went out, closing the door carefully behind them. The wooden garden gate creaked as it always did and Nuala glanced back anxiously.

"Garry," she exclaimed, putting her hand on his arm, "we've left the light burning!"

"Gosh!" the boy muttered. "I can't go back now. Let's leave it. What difference will it make?"

As they went down the road which skirted the bay Garry kept looking back.

"While the light is shining Gran hasn't found

out we've gone!" Nuala told him.

He shook his head.

"Gran won't come down, put out the light and go up again. She'll look in our rooms, find out we're gone and then—"

"Then what?" asked Nuala.

Garry clutched her arm.

"Don't think about it—we've started. We must keep on. Watch out now. We'll climb down to the shore road. No one would ever dream we'd do that. You hold on to Danny. I'll take care of Peter."

The moon was shining directly on the narrow footpath leading from the high road to the shore road.

"This is the best way, isn't it?" asked Nuala anxiously.

"It is," agreed the boy. "And if we're followed and have to hide there are caves among the rocks. Don't you remember that lovely one Gran found the last time Daddy was home for a fortnight."

"You mean that day when the storm came on and we had to shelter?" asked Nuala.

"That's it," declared Garry. "We had a picnic and Daddy built a big fire with driftwood."

"Will we have a picnic soon?" asked Peter. "I'm hungry!"

"You can't be hungry," his sister told him. "It's not long since we had supper. You must wait till it's time for breakfast."

"I'm sleepy," declared Danny. "Can't I go back to bed?"

"No, you can't!" snapped Garry. "If one of you grumbles or whines again, we'll leave you and you can find your way home alone."

"Don't frighten them," whispered Nuala. "Remember, they're only little ones."

"Tired," sighed Danny.

"Walk between us and hold our hands," Nuala told him. "Presently we'll come to a nice dry cave and we can rest for a while."

"And have our supper?" asked Peter hopefully.

Nuala sighed.

"You've had your supper," said Garry.

"Breakfast soon?" suggested Danny.

"When the sun rises," promised Nuala. "You can't possibly eat your breakfast till it's morning."

"Will Gran make toast?" Peter wanted to know.

Nuala pretended not to hear and Garry set off running.

"We'll race them!" he told Peter, pulling the little fellow along with him. But soon he stopped to let the others catch up.

"Are we anywhere near the caves?" asked Nuala.

"Don't you begin!" snapped Garry.

Nuala knew he was wishing they had stayed at home and she went on in silence.

"It's all my fault," she told herself. "If I had just gone to bed Garry wouldn't have thought of running away. But when we get to Castle Moat everything will be different."

Danny and Peter were weary and yawning, their feet stumbled on the stones. Even Nuala's eyes were closing and she felt she could not walk another step.

"We're there!" said Garry. "Look—there's the first cave."

"But the sea is flowing right up there," objected Nuala. "The waves are dashing against the rocks and pouring in the mouth of the cave."

They stopped suddenly.

"I'd forgotten the sea came in that far with the tide," muttered Garry. "We'll have to go over the rocks. But how can we? The two of us might manage it alone but not with these."

"Let's take the way across the bog," suggested his sister. "We can follow the cart tracks. Most likely we can shelter in one of the turf-cutters' huts when we get tired. We could light a fire."

The moon shone on the tossing waves, which sparkled as though tipped with diamonds. Inland the land lay dark and confused. Here and there Garry could make out vague shapes rising against the sky. These might be huts, clumps of trees or merely heaps of turf sods stacked up on the flat bog, waiting to be taken away.

His eyes were very sharp, but when Nuala looked in the same direction the sky and earth were all blurred and vague.

At that moment if her brother had suggested going back she would have agreed. Yet Garry was beginning to feel thrilled with the adventure. The breeze blew the fragrant smell of the cut turf into his face and he sniffed it with pleasure.

"Do you remember when Micky Reardon's dad took him turf-cutting in the holidays? They slept in a hut down below Slieve Beg—the little mountain—and he told me there was a fire there that hadn't been out for a year, maybe longer. Micky said it was grand and he'd ask his dad to let me come next holiday!"

"How shall we go?" asked Nuala practically. "Can we get up there without having to go back?"

"You wait here," Garry told her. "Sit down and rest while I do a bit of exploring."

"Want to come too!" clamoured Danny, clutching at his brother's hand.

"Sit down, you, and wait!" ordered Garry, giving the younger boy a push which sent him sprawling.

Without waiting to pick him up Garry scrambled over the rocks towards the dark bog and, almost at once, he vanished from sight.

Nuala didn't blame Garry for being impatient. She felt she had acted foolishly and had brought them all into trouble. But she was thankful to have him with her. She sympathised with Danny, who began to cry as if he had been badly hurt.

"That fella is only letting-on!" said Peter. "He's bigger than me, and there he is crying like a babby!"

"Don't be unkind!" Nuala reproved him. "Garry didn't mean to hurt him, but he did push him over. Now let us try to follow Garry so that he won't have to come back so far."

The two little boys were very tired, their eyes

were blinking but they were ready to try. Their sister coaxed them over the rocks to a soft patch of dry grass. When they reached it they settled down, and she was only too pleased to rest with them.

Her eyes were closing when a startled cry, "Nuala, where are you?" roused her to wakefulness.

"Here we are!" she called as her brother arrived and pulled her to her feet.

"We're in luck!" he cried excitedly. "There's a real hut over there and we can rest as long as we like. No one will come near it till the morning, that's sure. You hang on to Peter. I'll bring Danny. Come on!"

The hut was made of brown turf sods and planks. The men working on the bog had left boots, lanterns, sacks. The wind was shut out and, in a few moments, the children had settled themselves comfortably.

Nuala pulled a sack over herself and looked round to see how her little brothers were going on. Garry had already tucked them up.

"We'll just have a bit of a snooze and then we'll keep straight on," he said. "Weren't we eejits not to think of this way? Fancy trying to go by the shore."

Nuala nodded.

"I'm not really very good at adventures," she thought. "But I am glad to have Garry with me. If only we could have left the young ones behind."

Her eyes closed and she slept as soundly as in

her snug bed at home.

Garry found it harder to sleep. He remembered how often his father had reminded him that he was the eldest and should set a good example.

"Nuala is always in a dream," his father said. "She is a good child, but she forgets. I trust you to be a help to your Grannie while I'm away!"

"We shouldn't have run away," thought the boy. "What will Gran think when she wakes up in the morning and finds we've gone? She'll be terribly upset. Oh, I do wish we were back!"

He blinked sleepily, settled himself more comfortably and there he was, as sound asleep as the others.

A little later Nuala woke.

"Why am I not in my own bed?" she thought. "I don't remember coming here. I must be dreaming."

She was so used to dreaming, even when she was wide awake, that this didn't bother her at all. She yawned, stretched, bumped into Peter, who grunted, opened his eyes, closed them again and rolled over. Now the four of them were sleeping soundly, having dreams that were nearly as good as the stories their grandmother was always telling them.

9

On the Bog

Garry was the first to wake properly in the hut on the bog. He was puzzled and blinked sleepily as a ray of sunlight cut through into the cabin.

"Where in the wide world am I?" he asked himself.

He saw Nuala lying on her back and smiling, though her eyes were closed. The little boys were snuggled up against one another, Peter with his thumb in his mouth.

"Four years old and he still sucks his thumb," muttered Garry in disgust. "Wonder what it's like outside?"

He went out quietly, not wanting to wake the others. The sun cast a golden veil over the wide brown stretches of the bog. On all sides were heaps of turf, the sods resembling big rough bars of chocolate.

Garry remembered how his father had told him of earlier years when the turf was cut by hand with a slane—one, two three strokes of the long-handled, sharp-bladed spade, a toss over the left shoulder of each soft, smooth, shining brick of turf, perfectly shaped. A good cutter would send it flying through the air—soft and damp, yet landing in his helper's hands unbroken. The women stood them on end, three leaning against one another, to dry and harden before they were carted away.

"Hard work! Back-breaking work!" Tim Brophy had told his son. "Like all the other jobs, there was less pay and longer hours. But it made men strong as horses."

A loaded lorry stood at the edge of the bog road. Garry stared at it, frowning.

"If we could get a lift we'd be made up," he told himself. "I wonder would the men take us? They wouldn't mind one or even two, but four's a bit of a crowd. Still, I can try. It's sure to be going through Castle Moat."

He went slowly back to the hut.

"Nuala," he said softly, bending over her, for he didn't want to wake his little brothers till he had to.

She opened her eyes at once.

"Listen," he whispered. "There's a loaded lorry outside, ready to go off. If we can get on that we'll be at Aunt Maureen's in next to no time. We'll have to hide. They'd never take four of us—they'd think we were running away."

"Aren't we?" asked Nuala, blinking a little, for her eyes didn't want to stay open.

"Of course we're not!" exclaimed the boy indignantly. "We're going to our own aunt and uncle. That can't be running away."

"'Spose not," agreed Nuala doubtfully. "I hope they'll not be cross with us."

Garry sat down, clasping his knees.

"You know what Aunt Maureen is like. She'll take our part. She always does. And Uncle Desmond, he'll just laugh and say: 'Those young ones! What will they be up to next?' I can hear him saying it!"

The way he mimicked his uncle made Nuala laugh so much that she woke the other two.

"You see!" whispered Garry. "I bet the first thing Peter will say is: 'I'm hungry!'"

Danny yawned, turned over on one elbow and gazed about him in bewilderment.

Peter didn't bother to open his eyes.

"Hungry!" he mumbled, licking his dry lips.

Garry thought he looked so funny that he lay back choking with laughter.

His two brothers looked at him in wonder.

"Where's Gran?" asked Danny.

That made Garry serious.

"We'd better have something to eat," he said to his sister. "Then we can hide in the lorry."

Peter and Danny thought it was wonderful to have biscuits, cheese and dates for breakfast. But they wanted milk and, though Garry was angry with them for making a fuss, Nuala felt so thirsty she was quite sympathetic.

All at once Garry cried out: "Will you look what's there."

He was pointing at the far corner of the hut.

In a basket, which was packed with brown-paper parcels, a big thermos flask was standing upright.

The younger boys stared without understanding.

"If only there's something in it," murmured Nuala.

Garry did not speak. He reached over and lifted it, knowing by its weight that it was full.

"Hope it's not soup," he thought, unscrewing the top. The fragrant steam of hot coffee rose in the air.

"My word!" chuckled the boy. "Aren't we the lucky ones!"

He gave Danny the first drink. It was hot and sweet, and it made the little boy feel wide awake. He wiped his mouth with the back of his hand, crossed his legs and smiled contentedly.

Next came Peter's turn.

"Want milk!" he grumbled.

"You can't have it," his big brother told him. "Hurry up or you'll have to take the last turn."

Peter sipped with maddening slowness. At last he was finished.

"Now it's your turn." said Garry to Nuala.

She drank as quickly as she could, for she did not want to keep Garry waiting. They had two long drinks each then they settled down to more biscuits, cheese and dates.

"This is a lovely breakfast," said Garry. "We are lucky. If only Uncle Desmond isn't too cross I do believe everything will turn out all right."

"How can it?" thought Nuala despondently.

"Nothing will ever be the same again."

Still, she did not feel nearly so unhappy now. She was very fond of her aunt and uncle, and a wish was rising in her mind that they would take not only herself and her brothers to live with them but might also find room for Gran Brophy.

"I would like Daddy too," she thought, "but I suppose now he has our stepmother he won't want us."

Garry, reaching down to pull her to her feet, was surprised to see her eyes sparkling and her lips smiling.

"She is really plucky," he thought.

"We must make sure we can't be seen," Garry warned the others. "Once we reach Castle Moat it won't matter—at least I hope it won't. Maybe they'll just tell us to run along home and they won't know where we came from."

He scrambled into the lorry. Nuala was almost as quick. But he had to pull Danny and Peter up after him. The lorry was well packed, but there was a space at one end where the four of them could stretch out.

"As soon as the men come keep absolutely quiet," ordered Garry. "There is only one road across the bog and with luck we'll be at Castle Moat before there's any trouble."

Nuala frowned.

"Gran gets up very early," she reminded him. "I hope she won't worry."

"There won't be time," answered the boy. "We'll

be at Castle Moat before dinner. Uncle Des will send word to the post office and Gran will know we're safe. She'll have nothing to worry about."

Nuala found this very comforting.

"I am glad Garry is with us," she thought.

Garry yawned.

"I'm still sleepy. Let's all shut our eyes and try to go to sleep, then we'll be so quiet the men won't see us."

"That will be grand," agreed Nuala.

As for the younger ones, they were already asleep.

Nuala curled into one corner, Garry into another. The young ones used them as cushions. A lark rose into the air singing so sweetly that not one of them moved. All four were sound asleep.

Two men tramped round the lorry, seeing that everything was in order. The children were so well hidden they did not dream they had four passengers.

"I'm parched," said the older man. "I could do with a sup of hot coffee. Good thing young Dave left our packs when he came along."

"Me too!" said the other. "And I could do with a sandwich. The missus was up late last night with one of the kids, so I told her not to bother about breakfast for me."

They went off to the hut. Jer Butler, the elder man, lifted the thermos. It felt light but he did not worry about this until he unscrewed the top.

"Not so full, Shaun Dempsey," he said. "I expect

your missus was too bothered about the young one to notice."

"Not her," cried Shaun. "I saw her fill it to the brim."

"Take a look then!" said Jer.

They both shook their heads in bewilderment, set to work on their sandwiches and shared what coffee there was.

"I wouldn't say anything about the thermos," said Jer. "Your young missus has enough trouble on her hands. Besides, it's my turn to bring along the coffee tomorrow."

The other nodded, put the thermos into the lorry, climbed aboard and, when Garry opened his eyes, he felt he was being bumped up and down.

"Lucky the turf is well packed," he thought, and went to sleep again.

Nuala was the next to wake. The lorry was bumping over a wide road. There were shops on each side.

"This isn't Castle Moat!" she told herself, frowning. "I wonder where we are? Weren't we silly not to make sure where the lorry was going before we started. But how could we?"

She turned over and lifted her head.

Shaun Dempsey was nearest to her. She could see his face, stern and troubled, for he was thinking of the sick child at home.

"He looks terribly cross," Nuala decided. "Perhaps we'd better keep quiet till the lorry stops. We might be able to creep out without him knowing."

She was still trying to make up her mind what they should do when the lorry stopped. Garry opened his eyes, saw his sister was awake, put his finger to his lips and shook his head.

The men were backing the lorry into a side turning. They jumped down and stood talking. Shaun, the younger one, strolled away. Jer took out his pipe and, while he was lighting it, Garry slipped to the ground. Nuala followed quickly. But the little boys were only half awake.

"Don't make a sound," whispered Nuala. "Garry will lift you down."

Danny allowed himself to be pulled to the ground, but Peter was always difficult in the morning.

"Want Grannie!" he muttered, yawning and rubbing his eyes.

Jer's pipe was beginning to draw. He took it from his mouth, shook his head and was about to think he had imagined the voice, which seemed to come from the turf piled at the side of the cart, when Peter clutched at the sods and sent half a dozen rattling to the road.

The turf-cutter was startled when a boy, dragging a smaller one with him, raced along the lane into the main street, followed by a girl and another boy.

"Young stowaways!" he chuckled. "Now when did they climb up and where are they going? There's something queer about this and I'm going to find out what it is."

He strode after the children, but by the time he reached the end of the lane they had disappeared in the morning crowd going to and from the station, hurrying to shops and offices, down to the river or the lake.

He walked slowly back, puzzling over the children's sudden appearance and wondering what he should do.

Just then Shaun came along looking very cheerful and whistling loudly.

"I've got good news," he said. "My young one is better and we won't have to worry any more."

By the time they had talked over this good news Jer had forgotten all about the uninvited passengers.

They were busy delivering the turf at Carragh, near Sligo. It was only later, when he went home and his little daughter Anda was setting out for school, that he remembered the other children.

"Wait a moment, Anda!" he called. "Haven't you got four children from one family—the Brophys—at your school? Their father is away most of the time and the grandmother looks after them. That's right, isn't it?"

Anda nodded.

"Yes, Daddy, the Brophys! Nuala is my best friend. Her grandmother tells them wonderful stories and she tells them all to me. They're better than any of the stories in the books."

"There are three boys as well as a little girl, aren't there?"

"Yes—there's Nuala and Garry, besides Peter and Danny. But they're very little and awful silly," she added scornfully.

"What's all this about?" asked Mrs Butler. "It's time Anda was off to school."

"Well, a queer thing happened this morning," said her husband. "When we stopped up in the lane four children, a girl and three boys, scrambled out of the lorry and raced away. Before I could stop them they were lost in the crowd. They must have been hiding in the turf. I think they stowed themselves away before we started and we didn't notice them. I don't know why but the biggest boy reminded me, somehow, of Tim Brophy."

"It sounds very queer indeed," agreed Mrs Butler.

She turned to her daughter.

"Is there any reason why the children should run away?" she asked. "Are they unkindly treated at home?"

Anda looked shocked.

"Their grannie's a darling!" she said softly. "She makes them lovely cakes and all kinds of good things. When their father comes home he brings them wonderful presents. I think they're lucky children!"

The three looked at one another.

"Then why should they run away?" asked Jer.

His wife stood up.

"Anda, let you run!" she cried. "I hear the bus. You'll catch it easily at Carragh Cross. Better tell Miss Florrie what you have heard, unless the

Brophys come to school as usual. But if they're there, say nothing!"

"Not to a soul," put in Jer. "But run."

Anda ran.

10

Where Are the Children?

Gran Brophy always woke at six o'clock—summer or winter.

"That gives me good time to get meself acquainted with the world before the others open their eyes," she told herself.

She lay listening to the birds, smiling at their sudden uproars, the scoldings, chatterings, and wishing they would sing now as in summer when, often, she was awakened by a golden song of beauty so challenging that all the other sounds died away, as if hens, cows, sheep and all the creatures whose day was also beginning, paused to listen to the tuneful little blackbird.

The old woman liked to remember her dreams too.

"'Tis like turning the pages of a story-book," she murmured. "By rights I should keep an exercise book handy and write them down. Only I'm no class of a scholar at all, God help me! I could tell them to Nuala and have her write them down for me. She's a great little scholar and she'd love to do it. Now what did I dream about?"

She sat up in bed and sighed.

"I know now—'twas about the swans—the Four Swans of Enchantment, the Children of Lir! And didn't I have to be giving it out to the young ones and their father planning to bring them home a stepmother. But how was I to know?

"Mebbe I only dreamed I told them that story," she said hopefully, closing her eyes tightly and lying down again. But she knew she hadn't dreamed it.

She sat up abruptly.

"How can I undo the mischief me foolishness may have caused?" Gran asked. "Children are that queer, a body must be very careful with them.

"Sitting still won't make matters any better," she decided. "I'd as well stir meself, get busy on me rightful jobs and mebbe a notion will come to me."

She washed and dressed quickly. Feeling a good deal more hopeful she ran up the short staircase to the boys' room. She tapped at the door then pushed it softly.

"If they're sound asleep I'll let them lie awhile," she murmured.

Her eyes opened wide when she saw the two empty, disordered beds.

"The young imps!" she chuckled. "'Tisn't often they're awake before me, and I never heard a sound."

She opened the other door and shook her head

in bewilderment, for Nuala's bed was empty and disordered too. She stood at the top of the staircase and called" "Garry! Nuala!"

There was no answer.

"Ah well! If the four of them are together, they'll not come to much harm," she reflected. "I'll go below and get on with the breakfast."

Yet when she opened the door of the big room and saw the lamp still burning she was troubled.

"Haven't I warned Nuala and Garry never to light the lamp. I don't know what's come over them. They don't usually get up to such allegations. To go out without telling me! It isn't like them!"

In her heart she knew what was wrong and felt a chill.

"I'm foolish to be troubled," she told herself. "Everything may turn out for the best. Why wouldn't it? We're not living in savage times. But I do wish I knew what the children are doing and where they are."

She turned out the lamp and went into the kitchen to prepare breakfast.

"When there's trouble afoot, what can help more than a cup of good, strong, hot tea," thought Gran Brophy, putting on the kettle.

She fixed up a tray for herself and opened the larder door. She lifted the lid of the bread bin and smiled. Yesterday evening she had put in a new loaf of bread. It was untouched. But a square piece of cake and a lump of cheese had disappeared, and several layers from the biscuit tin had gone with them.

"Thanks be, they won't starve," she said, trying to laugh. "Now where can they have gone?"

She stood wondering and pondering, then she nodded.

"They'd make for their aunt's place. Haven't they always run to her when they were in trouble and I was not here to help? I'm surprised at Nuala taking the two young ones. But mebbe the little fellows wouldn't be left behind. I'll ask Dan the Post to keep an eye open for them if he has a letter for any of the coast houses."

She looked out from the window facing the shore. The waves were crashing against the rocks, flinging showers of spray into the air.

"They'd never get by that way," she decided. "The shore road will be covered. Nuala and Garry might manage it, but Danny and Peter wouldn't have a chance. Thanks be, the bog road is safe enough, if they go that way, though it's desperate long."

The kettle boiled and she made a pot of tea. She had no wish for food but, after a second cup of strong tea, she began to feel more hopeful.

"If only I can get them back before their father returns it won't be too bad. But it's no use me trying to take the shore road. I'd best go into the village and see if anyone is crossing the bog. A lift would make a deal of difference."

She was a quick walker and few of the doors and windows in the village were open when she arrived. The post office, which also sold newspapers, sweets, biscuits, bottles of mineral, writing-paper and envelopes, was the only shop really ready for customers. Dan the Post was standing at the counter, filling his bag and talking to the postmistress, Miss O'Shaughnessy, a girl from Sligo.

They both looked up in surprise at Mrs Brophy. It wasn't often she appeared in the village so early.

The postman shook his head.

"No letters for you today, Mrs Brophy, ma'am!" he told her.

"I was wondering if you had any letters for across the bog," she said.

Dan the Post laughed.

"Now isn't that queer! I have one for the aunt over at Castle Moat. A grand flat one it is and in Mr Brophy's writing—I'd know that writing a mile off! I'll be taking the letter over in another five minutes. Were you wishful to send a message?"

Mrs Brophy thought quickly. She hated making a fuss, and she knew that if the children had gone to Castle Moat their uncle would send back a message to her and bring them home as soon as he could. She had nothing to worry about.

"But supposing they hadn't gone there!" The thought crossed her mind. She shrugged her shoulders. "Where else could they go, especially with the two young ones?"

"Tell him I'd be glad if they'd come over today. There's something I'd like to discuss with them. Would you do that?"

"Why wouldn't I?" said Dan. "I'm always willing to do a message for a neighbour, especially when that neighbour is yourself, Mrs Brophy."

His friendliness cheered her, and when the post-mistress opened a new jar of milky mints and held it out, she slipped one of the fragrant sweets into her mouth and felt comforted.

"I'll call in on me way back," the postman said over his shoulder, letting the door slam behind him as he went off whistling.

"I hate the way Dan always lets the door bang," complained Miss O'Shaughnessy. "I've put in a demand for a spring. You know, one of those which makes a door close gently. They've promised it for ages and ages but it's never arrived."

Mrs Brophy did not hear her. She was wondering what she should do till the postman returned.

The young postmistress gave her a sharp, inquiring look.

"Is there anything bothering you, Mrs Brophy?" she asked. "Nothing wrong with the children, is there?"

The old woman hesitated. Suddenly she made up her mind. She felt she must tell someone. She leaned over the counter.

"I don't know," she answered. "I just don't know! When I went up to call them their beds were empty. They've left the house. They've disappeared and I don't know where they've gone."

Miss O'Shaughnessy's big brown eyes opened wide.

"Do you mean they've run away?" she asked in amazement.

Mrs Brophy nodded miserably. She felt almost ashamed.

The postmistress lifted the flap of the counter, came through and put a comforting arm round the old woman's thin shoulders.

"Why?" she asked. "Were you cross with them? That would upset them, especially Nuala. She's so fond of you."

Mrs Brophy shook her head.

"No, I wasn't cross with them. But I'm afraid it's all my fault. Listen, I'll tell you how it was."

"Sit down," said Miss O'Shaughnessy, drawing her companion on to the seat which ran along the wall near the door.

It was hard for Mrs Brophy to explain. She felt she was blaming her son and the stranger girl for something they knew nothing about, and she hated being unfair.

Miss O'Shaughnessy's eyes grew wider and wider as she listened.

"Don't worry yourself," she said consolingly. "I was often sorry for Tim and for you. You've had a hard time bringing up those four children since their mother died, and he away so often. I'm sure the girl he'd like is good and kind. You'll all be happy together and she'll be like a daughter to you.

"And don't worry about those young ones. They've most likely set out across the bog to go to their uncle. I'll tell everyone that comes in here to keep a look-out and they'll be brought back before the day's much older. I'll put a notice in the window if you like."

She put her head on one side and looked at Mrs Brophy with her bright, dancing eyes.

The old woman was horrified.

"No, no!" she cried. "I wouldn't want the children to be made a show of, and Tim would hate it."

Miss O'Shaughnessy sighed. She loved printing notices in red, black and blue ink. But she did not persist.

"Go home now and make yourself a nice strong cup of tea," she said. "Don't trouble another moment. Remember, we'll all be watching out. If the children are not back by dark, I'll send a search party out after them, I promise!"

"You're very kind," whispered Mrs Brophy. "You've given me great comfort."

The postmistress opened the door and bowed her out as she only did for her grand customers and best friends.

"I wish Tim was here," thought Mrs Brophy. "If he were home all my troubles would be ended."

The village seemed strangely deserted as she went back.

She took off her outdoor clothes and hung them in the hall.

"If I hadn't had two cups of tea already, I'd have one now," she said aloud. "But I could eat a slice of toast."

She made some toast and, without thinking, poured herself a cup of tea from the pot she had left on the hearth. Luckily it was still hot, though a trifle stewed.

As she leaned back in the comfortable armchair her eyes rested on her son's letter, which she had thrust behind the clock.

She frowned.

"There's the cause of all the trouble. If only that hadn't come we'd all be happy and contented, with the children safe at home."

11

Nuala's Friend

"I know I shouldn't be thinking that way," Mrs Brophy said aloud. "Hasn't Tim the right to a life of his own? I'm the one to blame—me and me story-telling! But how was I to know? If I'd only half a notion!

"Let me get the children back before Himself and the poor girl arrive—that's all I ask." The old woman's thoughts wandered on. "What's this her name is? Eva! Eva O'Mahony—and now she's Eva Brophy. I do hope she'll be happy. That will help the children. Now, why didn't he tell me?"

She opened the front door and gazed out.

The sky was grey, with low hanging clouds. The dark green waves were edged with delicate flounces of tossing foam.

"Thanks be it isn't raining," she murmured. "I wonder now, did they take their macs?"

She looked in the clothes cupboard. The children's macs were hung up on one big hook in the corner. She sighed, but this quickly turned to a smile.

"Ah well, haven't they their good coats? And, if it rains, they'll find shelter. But I do wish they'd taken their macs. And I hate them to miss school."

She sat down in her chair close to the fire. The room was warm yet she felt half frozen. When Boots jumped on her lap and looked up at her sideways, to see was he welcome, she stroked him firmly from his ears to the tip of his tail.

"You're a decent little fellow," she told him.

Mrs Brophy didn't mean to close her eyes, but she fell asleep and was dreaming that she was driving across the bog on one of the old sidecars when a continuous tap-tapping at the outer door roused her.

She blinked but sat still, not sure where she was.

The tapping came again and a cautious voice called softly: "Are you there, Mrs Brophy? It's me, Anda Butler—Nuala's friend!"

"Ah, the little fair girl," murmured the old woman, waking up. Raising her voice she said, "Come in, pet. Close the door behind you."

A child, so fair, slight and dainty, her mother had a secret fear she might be taken away by the Good People, came in on tiptoe.

"I do hope I'm not disturbing you," she almost whispered, "but me daddy said I was to come in and tell you before I went to school. He said Miss Florrie wouldn't be cross with me for being late when she knew he'd sent me with a message to you."

Mrs Brophy opened her eyes wide and sat up

straight. The big black cat had to dig his claws into her frock to prevent himself from being toppled on the floor. She pressed him back gently.

"A message!" she repeated. "Is it about the children?"

Anda tiptoed across the room nodding, and tossed back her cloud of golden hair. She paused to stroke Boots who purred complacently.

"Daddy thinks that Nuala and the boys are safe. He believes they slept in the turf hut and scrambled into the turf lorry. They jumped out and ran way when the lorry came to Carragh. We live there and sometimes, when I don't come by bus, he brings me to school in the lorry. He sent me to tell you. But I must run now or Miss Florrie will be cross with me."

She stepped away, opened the door and was gone before Mrs Brophy could stop her. But the old woman didn't mind. At least she knew the children were safe. But where were they? Now where did that fair child live? Nuala was always chattering about her friend Anda, the prettiest girl in the school. But if she had ever mentioned where Anda lived Mrs Brophy had forgotten.

"No! Of course, hadn't Anda herself said she lived at Carragh, which was close to Sligo. But what in the wide world were the children doing there?"

"You needn't grumble—you shall have your bread and milk," she told the cat. "Eat it up quickly, for I'm in a hurry! And you'll not want to be left shut up on your lone in the house."

She felt almost cheerful as she took the shortest way to the school, over the stile, through the wood and out beyond the village.

The school was a new one and the people of Craigcullen were very proud of it and of the well-equipped playground, which had a swing and a see-saw, as well as a giant's stride for the boys and the more venturesome girls.

Mrs Brophy stood for a moment.

"Isn't it good to be young nowadays," she thought. "And, 'pon me word, it's not too bad for us old ones either. Isn't it grand to know the hard days are over—no canes or straps now, not in our school anyway! And no keepings-in unless a boy or a girl is very bold. Everyone is learning a deal more than they used to."

She pushed open the gate of the playground and crossed to the school door. The children were singing "Out and Make Way for the Bold Fenian Men!"

Mrs Brophy stood still, listening and smiling.

"They were grand fellas, no doubt," she told herself. "But I'm glad there's an end to the fighting and heartbreak."

The singing ceased. There was silence, broken only by a scraping of boots on the floor. She went in quickly, closed the door and stood with her back to it, gazing at the faces of the children and their teacher.

"You wish to speak to me?" asked Miss Florrie

Lewis, pushing back her dark curly hair.

"I do indeed," said Mrs Brophy eagerly. "That is, if I'm not intruding," she added politely.

"Not at all," said the young teacher. She turned to the class. "Go on with the sum written on the board. I trust you all to be quiet while I'm speaking with our visitor."

'That one isn't a visitor," whispered one of the boys. "She is the Brophys' grannie. It's the first time they've ever been absent."

"Is it about the children?" asked the teacher. "Nothing serious, I hope? I missed them this morning."

"No use trying to keep a secret in Craigcullen," decided Mrs Brophy, and she told the teacher the whole story.

"That little fair girl—she's a great friend of Nuala's—ran in to tell me they were safe," went on Mrs Brophy. "She was off before I could ask her where her father saw them. So I came here to see if you could help me."

"Of course I'll do everything I can," declared Miss Florrie.

She beckoned to the little fair girl, who came running.

"Tell Mrs Brophy all you know about Nuala and the other children, Anda," said Miss Florrie. "Where did your father see them and when?"

Anda had listened carefully to her father telling her mother about the four children who had hidden in the turf cart. Now, feeling very excited and important, she repeated all he had said.

The teacher and the old woman looked at one another. Mrs Brophy drew a deep, thankful sigh.

"They can't be far away," she declared. "Where exactly do you live, dear? It's in Carragh, isn't it?"

Anda nodded.

"It's near Sligo and I come in every day on the bus, except when Daddy brings me. It stops at our corner, at Carragh crossroads."

Mrs Brophy knew very little about that side of the county, but the fact that Anda didn't live very far away seemed to bring the runaways nearer.

"It might be best for you to go to the Garda station," advised Miss Florrie. "The Garda have a fast car. They can whizz all over the countryside and you can stay here. Or would you sooner go home? The moment there's any news I'll send one of the children to you."

"And the police will put out posters!" murmured the old woman bitterly. "A queer homecoming for my poor son and the girl he's bringing back with him."

The young teacher's eyes opened wide.

"I don't understand!" she exclaimed. "Do you mean he's bringing back a stepmother for the children?"

Mrs Brophy nodded mournfully.

"And isn't it queer now! I tell the children a story most nights before they go to bed and— would you believe it—last night if I didn't tell them the legend of the Children of Lir! I expect you know it! Mebbe someone sent you to bed when you were a child with your heart aching for their sorrows."

Miss Florrie shook her head.

"Nobody told me stories—I wish they had. But I was given a book of Irish legends on my eleventh birthday. Even now I remember how I sat up in bed reading about the poor Swan Children, and how I cried myself to sleep!"

"But you had your own mother to comfort you," sighed the old woman.

Miss Florrie shook her head again.

"My mother didn't approve of such stories, so I didn't tell her what was troubling me. My favourite uncle gave me the book, and he never knew how he nearly broke my heart—not permanently of course!"

Miss Florrie laughed, and Mrs Brophy, for all her trouble, found herself laughing with her. She stood up, thanked the teacher and turned away.

"Wait!" exclaimed Miss Florrie. "I'll send a note to the post office, asking Miss O'Shaughnessy to phone the Garda. They'll find the children for you quickly and bring them back."

Mrs Brophy swung round.

"Is it put the Garda on the poor children?" she cried in horror. "Their father would never forgive me!"

Miss Florrie stood looking at her in silence.

"The quicker they're found the better!" she said very firmly. "You wouldn't want their father to come back before they're home, would you now?"

The old woman sighed.

"You're right," she said. "Me and me stories! Why didn't I let them wait until they were old enough to enjoy reading the legends for themselves. I've been very foolish—but I didn't know how things were going to turn out, did I?"

Mrs Brophy went away from the school smiling to herself. Miss Florrie made her feel that her troubles were nearly over and the children would soon be back. Everybody she met seemed to be in a good temper. The sun was shining. The breeze was gentle and, by the time she reached home, she wouldn't have been a bit surprised to find the children indoors, waiting for her and wondering where she was.

But they weren't.

12

No News Is Good News— Sometimes!

Gran Brophy gave the house a good cleaning. She usually started on Saturday morning, so that by Sunday there was a gleam on floors and furniture. She loved sweeping, she loved polishing and she so loved hot, soapy water, she was always willing to let the children blow bubbles.

While she waited to hear from the aunt and uncle over at Castle Moat, she tried to imagine what they would say when they heard the children had run away. She could not think of anywhere else they would go.

"Aunt Maureen was always terribly fond of Nuala's mother," she mused. "They were more like sisters than friends. Whenever she looks at the young one Maureen sees her mother. She'll be very upset when she hears that Nuala has run away. I wouldn't be surprised if she blames me. Don't I blame meself!

"It made her aunt happy to see Nuala growing more like her mother every day. She may take it hard when she hears of a stepmother coming in to the place, though if it turns out better for the children that should comfort her as well as me. In any case I know she'll try to make the best of things. But why didn't Tim give us all a chance to prepare ourselves as well as the children? I do wish! What do I wish?"

When it was time for Dan the Post to call, she went out to the gate. She could see and hear him in the distance, proudly riding his new motorcycle. As he came nearer, shaking his head, it was plain to see he had no news.

"The Devlins—at Castle Moat—haven't set eyes on them!" he called. "Nor has anyone else!"

"Where can they have gone?" she cried in despair, clasping her hands together. "What in the world should I do?"

"Himself, Mr Devlin, rang up the Garda station," Dan told her. "They promised, as soon as they hear anything, to phone the post office here. If I'm not around when the message comes Miss O'Shaughnessy will get one of the lads to bring it along."

"But where can they have gone?" cried Mrs Brophy again, her eyes wide with anxiety. "Thank God the four of them are together! Garry should have had more sense. How could he run off with those two little ones? And Nuala has always been such a sensible child. What can have come over her?"

"If ye ax me, ma'am, twasn't the lad, but young

Nuala herself that's to blame. Most likely Garry went to look after her and then them two little imps wouldn't be left behind," declared Dan.

They stood looking at one another for a moment. Gran's face was pale, her eyes anxious. She feared every kind of disaster and blamed herself.

"After all," said Dan comfortingly, "this isn't Darkest Africa—this is Ireland, a Christian country. They'll soon be tired of running round on their own, and they can't move far or fast with the young ones. If they don't come back, they'll be brought back by the polis. Of course there's the disgrace," he added, nodding thoughtfully. "People will want to know what reason they had to run off."

"Disgrace!" echoed Mrs Brophy scornfully. "Where's the disgrace if they come back! This is the one thing that matters now! Aren't we all foolish sometimes? You will let me know, if you can, the moment you hear a word, won't you, Dan?"

"I will so!" he assured her. "I wouldn't want you to be vexing yourself a moment longer than need be. Though there's nothing really to be anxious about. Garry's a fine strong lad and Nuala is really a sensible young girl, even if this doesn't seem a very sensible thing to do!"

Dan jumped on his bicycle and went off while she went back to the kitchen.

"I'd best have a good meal ready, whatever happens," Mrs Brophy informed Boots. "And the

day Tim brings his bride home I'll do a bit of
cooking that will make the pair of them open their
eyes. If only the children are home by then! But
what will I say to them? Ah, let the children only
come back unharmed and I'll not be dumb. I won't
be cross. I'll just talk good common sense and
kindness. That's a medicine can't be beaten. Dan
the Post is right to wonder what made them run
away. They'll never think it all arose out of an
ancient story."

Boots purred in agreement and Mrs Brophy,
who thought work and a cup of hot strong tea the
best cure for all troubles, filled the big kettle, put
it on the hob, gathered up her long stiff broom,
the short soft hand-brush, the dust-pan, a tin of
polish and a big thick rag.

She carried these to the top of the house, ready
to clean the whole place from top to bottom, and
then returned to make the pot of tea.

There were special occasions when Boots was
treated to a sweet milky saucer of tea. This happened
now!

Boots lapped busily, his pink tongue going in
and out. The old lady sipped her tea. Her big cup
and his saucer were finished at the same time. She
piled the crocks in the sink and went upstairs to
begin work.

"I'll put the children out of me mind until I
have the place looking as if it had been built and
furnished only this morning," she told herself.

She cleaned every window, dusted every piece

of furniture, polished the stairs and floors then, tired out, sat in her armchair by the fire.

She picked up the book she had brought from the village library the last time she went there. She read the title, *Knocknagow, or The Homes of Tipperary*. She had not had a chance yet to turn the first page.

"You'd think I'd have read this years ago," she murmured. "But when do I have time for a bit of reading, barring the paper?"

She leaned back, with the closed book on her knee.

"I don't seem to be able to read," she told the cat, who sat bolt upright on the hearthrug, letting his claws go in and out, but not purring.

He watched the mistress of the house anxiously, as if he knew she was in trouble.

"You do know there's something wrong, don't you, Boots?" she said. "'Tis the children, God help them! How can I concern meself with the troubles of people in a story when I'm faced with desperate trouble of me own?

"If they come home safe," she reflected, "I'll never grumble again. I'll never worry whatever happens. If there's quarrels I'll make peace. I'll spend the rest of me life endeavouring to let nothing but happiness inside this door. Dear, oh dear! Why didn't I wake up when they were going out? Me—that's always boasting what a light sleeper I am!"

She shook her head, pressed her lips together

and stood up.

"I shouldn't worry too much," she said. "Aren't the Garda on the job? Aren't they the men to find out everything that's lost? And they'll let the post office know the minute they have news. But perhaps Miss O'Shaughnessy mightn't have anyone handy to send out when she does hear! Why should I sit here when good news might have come through with no one there to bring it! What's to stop me from going along and finding out the news this very minute?"

She pulled on her boots and her long coat. "I might get a jar of blackcurrant jam and a few other things," she thought. "'Twill be a bit of a treat for the young villains when they do come home, whether they deserve it or not."

She opened the street door and, while she was standing there, looking round to make sure that everything was in order—the fire, the pile of turf, the kettle—Boots slipped past her and stood waiting on the path.

"Mebbe you're better out in the open," she told him. "Only don't you go running off!"

Mrs Brophy was always a quick walker. She closed the gate behind her and set off as fast as she could. She came out on the main road and looked towards the village.

"I've never seen the place so empty before," she said to herself. "If I'm in a hurry there's always someone ready to pass the time of day, wanting to tell me the news even if there isn't any, and longing to ask my opinion of the neighbours, the weather, or anything that might be happening. Now they're all hiding themselves as if they couldn't bear to set eyes on me. What ails the place, I'd like to know?"

She turned off by the old oak tree to the side road leading to the centre of the village. Suddenly she stopped. There was a look of desperation on her face. Coming towards her was Mrs Cronin, well known in the village as a woman who never took a cheerful view. And Mrs Brophy felt that just now she needed all the comfort she could get.

"No, I couldn't put up with that old angashore, not now! She always looks on the black side of everything and she'd drive me mad!"

She was about to return to the main road, to take the long way round, when the small neat figure of a woman dressed in brown caught up with the tall angular woman in black, who was walking quickly towards her.

"Good morning!" they called as they drew near to Mrs Brophy.

"Any news?" asked the small woman.

"If there is," said the tall woman in black sorrowfully, "'tis more than likely to be bad news. But I hope it's not too serious."

She put her head on one side. "Just like an old crow!" thought Mrs Brophy bitterly.

Before she could answer, Mrs Cadogan, the little woman in brown, turned to her.

"You might have reason to fret if it was only

one of the children missing," she said, "but when there are the four of them, I don't see how they could come to much harm. I'm perfectly sure they'll come home all right, a bit scared perhaps and very sorry to have caused you all this trouble."

Her bright eyes were like a bird's and her words were a comfort.

"I do believe you have the rights of it," Mrs Brophy said. "They are good children. I'm inclined to worry if things go the least bit wrong. You've cheered me up and I'm very grateful. All the same I'll go to the village and see if there's any tidings."

"Prepare yerself for the worst!" Mrs Cronin, the woman in black, advised her in sombre tones. "If there's nothing wrong, why hasn't someone seen them? Wouldn't they go straight to the polis? Doesn't it stand to reason? And if by any chance they do come back unharmed, let it be a warning to ye—ye're a great deal too soft with the four of them. I know them—talking back and answering up as if they were grown men and women!"

"But they're never rude, are they now?" protested Mrs Brophy. "I can't believe they're rude."

"Indeed they're not!" cried little Mrs Cadogan. "I've never know better behaved children in me life. When they do come back, and you have an evening to spare, bring them to tea. I'll make some of my special mince-pies, even if it isn't Christmas!"

By the time this was settled Mrs Cronin had grown tired of the talk and had marched off with her head in the air, still looking mournful. So Mrs

Cadogan said she would go back to the village with Mrs Brophy to hear if there was any news of the children.

Mrs Brophy told the kind little woman of her son's marriage.

"A stepmother!" said Mrs Cadogan. "That explains everything! The children were afraid! They didn't know there can be good as well as bad stepmothers. It does seem as though someone had been telling them foolish stories. I wonder who it could be?"

Mrs Brophy sighed.

"I'm afraid I'm the one. I often tell them a story before they go to bed, and the night before last I told them about the Children of Lir and how their wicked stepmother changed them into swans. When the storm came on there were four big swans out on the bay. 'Twas them started me off. Then the letter came. I can tell you I wished I hadn't been so foolish. But how was I to know?"

Little Mrs Cadogan looked troubled.

"What else could you do? Besides, I expect you were flummoxed!"

Mrs Brophy stood still.

"I was flummoxed, I can tell you! But I was glad for Tim's sake. Only now it'll be a bit of an up-heaval."

The two women walked on. The story was finished as they reached the post office.

"I wonder what will be the best way to set about it all?" murmured Mrs Cadogan, shaking her head. "Now where would the children be most likely to go? What about the aunt and uncle at Castle Moat? The children are fond of them, aren't they?"

Mrs Brophy nodded.

"They are indeed. But Dan the Post went over there to find out if the children had arrived. The Devlins hadn't set eyes on them since I took them over last Sunday. They sent word they'd come as soon as they could manage it."

Mrs Cadogan laid her hand on her companion's arm.

"Listen now," she said. "There's no doubt the story, with the letter coming on top of it, frightened Nuala. She's a dreamy child and a story like that would seem very real. But she'd trust you and her father. Soon enough she'll understand that she's been very foolish to run away. Besides, it's so long since her own mother died, and Nuala was such a little scrap, she could hardly remember her."

"I'm not so sure," replied Mrs Brophy. "I couldn't bear poor Cathleen to be forgotten. She was so good to me and I was very fond of her. I was always talking about her to the children. I see now 'twas selfish of me. The poor girl that's coming here has a strong memory to contend with and 'tis my fault."

Mrs Cadogan screwed up her thin little face.

"Don't tell me there isn't room in Nuala's heart for the old and the new. If the girl that's coming is good and sensible, she won't blame the child, and she'll have you to help her. Get the children back and we'll all rally round."

Mrs Brophy's eyes brightened.

"You're right," she declared. "Tim is a good lad. He'll have put the girl wise to the way things are and when—soon, I hope—I have the children back, they'll surely take a liking to her! I'll have a good talk with Nuala. I'm very glad I could talk it over with you. Now I'm off to find out what I can. Someone must have seen the children somewhere."

Mrs Brophy went to the post office. Mrs Cadogan walked on to the stores. Both shops were crowded and everyone was talking about the Brophy children. She stood just beside the open door of the post office and listened sorrowfully.

"No news," she decided. "I couldn't bear to stay here, listening to all that old chat, though I'm sure they mean it well. If only I can get the children back before Tim and their new mother comes. What a beginning for that poor girl! I'm beginning to be sorry for her too. Still, something may have happened to the children! If only I knew which way to turn! All this time I've been worrying about what I should tell them. But now all I'm longing for is to have them home with me. Come back safe, ye little ruffians, and I'll never find fault with ye again!"

13

On the Road

Garry stared at the jumble of motor-cars, horse-drawn vans, bicycles and the surge of pedestrians who, each and every one of them, seemed determined to push the four young wanderers into the gutter.

He had never realised before what a number of people there were in the world. Clutching Danny's hand he tried to go as quickly as if he were in the quiet little village of Craigcullen.

"Even on fair day its never as crowded as this," he thought. "Where can we be?"

His eyes, looking anxiously along the street of shops, at last made out a name over a square grey building with swinging doors, which were opening and shutting unceasingly—backwards and forwards, backwards and forwards.

Above the central narrow window in plain black letters, the boy read—"Sligo."

"Dad's been here!" he said aloud.

At once he felt less strange. In any of the draper's shops there must be someone who knew his father. If he could only speak to one of them. He glanced at his sister. He knew that wide, solemn look in her eyes. She was frightened and trying not to show it.

"Nuala," he said softly, "what shall we do now? We must have come the wrong way."

"A bus does go near Castle Moat," she answered. "Look at all the buses here. One of them must go there. I've often heard Aunt Maureen say she comes shopping here. If we get the right bus we'll be with Aunt Maureen and Uncle Des before dinner time. I suppose we'd better ask."

The boy nodded.

He saw a fat, good-humoured looking man strolling along, avoiding hurrying passers-by, without apparently seeing them stopping now and again to gaze in a shop window, and whistling softly as though perfectly content with life.

"That's the one," thought Garry.

"'Scuse me, sir," he said politely, standing in front of the man, "can you tell me where we'll get the bus to Castle Moat crossroads?"

The man stared down at him.

"Castle Moat!" he repeated. "Never heard of the place. You see, laddie, I'm a stranger here. I'm from the States. Wasn't even born here. Just looking round where I imagine my ancestors used to come on market day—but wait. Here comes one of those chaps they call garda. He'll tell us! Hi, sir, d'ye mind telling this lad where to get the bus to Castle Moat?—Here—what's wrong?"

Nuala had grabbed her brother.

"Don't wait!" she cried. "Run!"

Garry frowned but obeyed. He wasn't sure he would be wise to tell the garda they had run away from home and had mitched from school as well.

So there the four were—running, dodging, bumping into indignant shoppers, until they turned down a side street and came into the market-place.

Danny and Peter thought this great fun, and when all four of them—puffing and panting—collapsed on a doorstep between sacks of potatoes, they laughed and punched one another without knowing why.

"Apple!" demanded Danny, pointing at a stall where the woman in charge was polishing her stock of big red eating applies with a crumpled-up newspaper.

"We may as well," said Garry. "I'm starving."

"We have biscuits and cheese," his sister reminded him.

"That's great," he told her. "We can eat them first and finish up with the apples."

The woman allowed him to pick out four of the biggest and charged only a penny each.

"That's good isn't it?" Garry asked Nuala.

But Nuala never knew the cost of anything. Even Gran Brophy thought it backward for a girl of her age.

"They're lovely apples," she said, plunging her sharp teeth into the one he gave her.

"Will we eat our biscuits now?" asked Garry

when he had finished his apple.

The fruit woman looked at them curiously.

"Shouldn't you young ones be in school?" she asked. "'Tisn't a holiday, is it?"

"'Tis at our school!" answered Garry quickly.

Nuala opened her eyes wide, but before she could speak Garry nudged her.

"Best be on our way," he whispered.

He grabbed Danny's hand and pulled him to his feet. They were once more hurrying without knowing where they were going, while the apple woman stared after them doubtfully.

"I hope those young ones know what they are up to," she said to herself. "It looks to me mighty like mitching, and it's when they're mitching that the accidents happen!"

A grown-up customer came along and the four children passed out of her mind.

"Tired!" said Danny.

"Want Grannie!" said Peter.

"Copy-cat!" jeered his big brother.

Peter's eyes filled with tears.

"Don't cry, there's a good boy," coaxed Nuala. "We're going on a bus ride to Aunt Maureen. Won't that be grand? We'll have dinner with them!"

"Apple pudding!" said Danny hopefully, his eyes shining.

"Most likely," his big sister told him.

They trotted along contentedly. On the outskirts of the market they saw a traveller caravan.

"Hooray! There's a signpost!" exclaimed Garry. "Now we can see our way!"

"We'll be in Castle Moat before their fair is well over," said a tall traveller as he stepped back to admire some repairs he had just done to the caravan. "I was afeard that confounded wheel would banjax us."

"And hasn't it?" grumbled a woman in a tattered shawl tucked around a baby she held in her arms.

Garry had often envied the travellers their carefree life. He stared now at the van with its ragged canvas cover, the unpainted body, the broken shafts, mended with broomsticks, fastened with string and rusty wire, and the poor, bony, grey-black mare, its head hanging down, munching her feed in an old canvas bag.

"They're going to Castle Moat," he thought. "That's where we want to be and the sooner the better."

He knew that Nuala was afraid of travellers, but if once they were in Castle Moat would it matter how they reached it?

"This is a chance to get there quickly," he whispered to her.

Nuala hadn't been listening. She was thinking how terrible it must be to live in this dirty, broken-down van, wandering through the country with no welcome anywhere. Yet the woman's face was round and friendly, the man's eyes had a merry twinkle and the baby sucked its thumb as though it was the sweetest thumb a baby could have.

When Garry put his hand on the shaft and asked as boldly as he could, "Would you please give us a lift to Castle Moat?" Nuala stood still and silent.

"What's that?" asked the man, staring at the children.

"They want a lift," the woman told him. "Mitching, I expect."

Nuala looked up at her as she sat holding the baby on the front seat of the caravan.

"We're going to me aunt and uncle's house in Castle Moat," she said indignantly.

"Are they watching out for you?" asked the man, taking a tin of tobacco from his pocket and rolling a cigarette with two fingers of one hand so quickly and neatly that Garry was astounded.

The woman laughed.

"Weren't you ever young?" she asked her husband.

"But four of them!" he protested. "Have sense, Maggie!"

"I don't mind making room for them," she chuckled, "and we'll soon find out if they're telling the truth."

"Of course we're telling the truth!" cried Garry. "But if you think we're telling lies, keep your old van to yourselves and we'll walk!"

"You two might manage the tramp to Castle Moat," said the woman calmly, "but not those little chaps. We'll take them, and if you're too grand to jump up alongside me you can hang on behind."

"We'll come with you," declared Garry hurriedly before Nuala could say anything. "And thank you very much."

The tall traveller swung Danny up and tucked him in safely at the woman's feet. Peter opened his mouth to protest, but found himself sprawling beside his brother. Nuala scrambled up, smiled shyly at the woman who gave her a friendly pat.

"I'll walk!" said Garry proudly. But there he was, between the two travellers, while the dingy grey horse, with a toss of its head, started off at once.

"Now tell us the whole story," ordered Maggie. "I do love a true story."

"Mind your own business," thought Garry. But the woman's eyes were so friendly, while the man looked as if he didn't care whether he heard the story or not, that the boy found himself telling what had happened without leaving a single thing out.

"I suppose you haven't a biscuit left?" asked the woman. "I do love a biscuit."

At once Garry opened the bag of provisions and there they sat eating biscuits, cheese, seed cake and dates. They washed this down with sips of hot strong travellers' tea from a billy can wrapped in an old jersey. They had plenty of sugar but no milk.

The jersey was as grubby as everything else, but the children, even Nuala, thought it was the best meal they had ever had. Danny and Peter soon went to sleep, their arms round each other.

"The dotes!" murmured Maggie. "'Pon me word! I wouldn't mind keeping those two."

Nuala sat up very straight.

"We wouldn't give Danny and Peter to anyone!" she declared. "Would we, Garry?"

"Rather not!" agreed her brother, though he couldn't help thinking that running away would be much simpler if there were only the two of them.

"I expect Nuala would be lonesome and so would I," he told himself.

Now they were coming to a fir wood where the road divided, one branch going out across the bog, the other rising to the castle ruins. Garry and Nuala knew where they were now.

"That's where our aunt and uncle live!" announced Garry, pointing to where a line of carts were parked against the trees. "Just beyond there."

The fair was held in the shelter of the castle wall, and the noise of buying and selling drifted back to them.

"Will ye be all right now?" asked the tall traveller. "If yer aunt and uncle happen to be out come back to us," Maggie told them. "If anything goes wrong, stay with us and we'll land ye back home before ye're really missed."

"Thanks awfully," said Garry, jumping down.

"I'll tell everyone how good and kind you've been," declared Nuala.

On their way to their uncle's house the children kept turning to wave farewell.

"'Pon me word, the people them young ones ran away from must be quare!" exclaimed Maggie. "I hate parting with them!"

She jumped to the ground, her husband tethered the horse, and soon the travellers and their baby were swallowed up in the crowds at the fair.

"Come along do!" grumbled Garry as his sister stood staring after the travellers. "They can look after themselves. We still have to find out what Aunt Maureen and Uncle Des will think of us running away."

"It's not really running away," insisted Nuala. "Not when we're going to relations."

"Who haven't asked us and mayn't want us," Garry said.

Nuala gazed at him blankly.

"Do you really think they mayn't want us?" she asked. "They always have wanted us. Don't you remember what a lovely time they gave us last Easter when Daddy was away? Gran had gone to stay with that friend of hers who was ill."

"That was different," said Garry. "Gran took the young ones with her. Aunt and Uncle had only the two of us, and Uncle Des said I was the best helper he'd ever had at stacking the turf."

Nuala tried to think of any particular way in which she had helped her aunt. But she couldn't.

"All I did was to sing for them," she said sadly.

Garry glanced at her mournful face.

"You sing jolly well," he told her kindly. "Here we are," he went on. "Now our troubles are over."

But the gate to the front garden was padlocked.

"Bother! They're out!" said Garry, turning to his sister. "What in the wide world has happened?"

"Maybe they're at the back and just fastened the gate to keep strangers out because of the fair. Come on, let's go round the back and see," suggested Nuala.

There was a high wall all round the low stone house, much too high for the young ones to get over.

"Where can they be?" wondered Garry.

"This has never happened before," said Nuala in dismay. "What shall we do?"

She sat on the grassy bank which bordered the land. The little boys flopped down beside her.

"Dinner," murmured Danny.

"Shut up, you!" said his big brother fiercely.

Garry was usually so good-tempered that both Danny and Peter stared at him open-mouthed, then they turned and hugged one another for comfort.

"Wish Grannie would come," sighed Peter.

Danny nodded.

"Wish we were home!" he whimpered.

"Do you think I like the way things are happening?" demanded Garry. "I do wish we'd never left home!"

Nuala was very nearly crying. She told herself she must be brave now. But a feeling of despair overwhelmed her. She sank down on the ground and burst into tears.

"Don't! Don't!" pleaded Garry. "I'm terribly sorry, Nuala. I didn't mean to make you cry. If you think it best we'll stay with the travellers' caravan till they come back or we'll go and look for them. I'll do anything you want."

Nuala dried her eyes.

"I'm sorry, Garry," she spluttered. "I never thought I'd be such a cry-baby. But nothing has turned out the way I thought it would. If only I'd come away alone you and the boys would be home now."

14

The Young Housebreakers

"Hallo there!" came a call from the road. "Anyone at home? Why, if it isn't the young Brophys! What are ye doing here at all? And where's the aunt and uncle?"

"We don't know," answered Garry dolefully. "We're waiting for them."

He stood up as Séamus Rafferty, the old ballad singer, came marching along, his grey curly hair tousled and windblown, his pack on his back, slashing with his blackthorn stick at the wayside nettles. Everybody in Craigcullen—old and young—knew Séamus Rafferty and he knew everybody. They thought he was the best ballad singer in all Ireland.

He sat down on the bank beside the children, rolled the two little boys on their backs so that they screamed with laughter. Then he looked up at the two bigger ones.

"Folks out?" he asked. "Didn't know you were coming, mebbe? At the fair, I suppose. Hope they won't be long. I could do with a sup of tay."

"Song!" demanded Danny.

"Song!" echoed Peter.

"In a minit," promised the ballad singer. "I want first of all to know what's going on here! I can see something's wrong. Tell me the trouble. You, young Nuala, speak first, as the only lady in the contraption."

At any other time Nuala would have been very flattered at being called a lady. Now she was too bothered and confused to be pleased at anything. She shook her head and looked away.

"How about *you* telling me what's up, Garry?" said Séamus. "I might be able to help. You know I'm your friend. You can trust me."

Garry looked questioningly at his sister. She nodded.

He told the whole story, right from the very beginning. When he mentioned the four swans, the ballad singer leaned forward, listening eagerly to every word. Suddenly Garry stopped.

"I can't go on!" he stuttered. "I can't!"

Séamus Rafferty looked from one young face to another. Even the little boys had grieved over the sorrows of the four Swan Children, condemned for so long to such suffering and wandering.

The ballad singer understood. How often had he held an audience silent and moved by that same story.

He nodded.

"Listen to me," he said. "I can understand how you felt, Nuala, and you with the same name as that poor child. But times have changed. Queer things do happen. But this business of the four swans couldn't happen today. And stepmothers needn't be cruel at all. You believe that, don't you, Garry?"

"I believe you," said the boy, looking straight at the ballad singer.

Séamus Rafferty settled himself more comfortably, unfastening his pack and laying it on the ground at his feet. He took out his pipe and, when it was pulling steadily, crossed his legs and began to talk as if to himself.

"Time was when I didn't hold with telling the ancient legends to everyone, young and old. Now I give out to all that will listen. The first time I heard the old stories meself I was like young Nuala here, I didn't consider the time or the place, what you might call the historical background.

"Now when you first went to school, Nuala, and heard all the strange things they do hand out, I'm sure you went home time out of mind to your grannie and lamented over what you'd heard. I remember when I first heard about the two little princes in the Tower of London, and their wicked uncle who had them killed, I nearly broke me heart over those young lads. Did you ever hear tell of them?"

He looked from Garry to Nuala. Garry nodded. Nuala looked puzzled.

"That's English history," said the boy. "It isn't in our book. But Mr Donnelly told us about it one day."

"Do you know any orphans who have such an uncle?" asked Séamus Rafferty, putting his head on one side.

"I know the Conlons—a boy and a girl—Kit Conlon is my friend. They are orphans," said Garry speaking very slowly. "They have an uncle and an aunt too, who wouldn't let anyone lay a finger on them. We have an uncle and aunt who live here but that isn't the same as a stepmother."

"Do you think it fair to judge someone you've never met by a legend about a person who lived long, long ago?" said Séamus, turning to Nuala. "I really am surprised at you, Nuala. I thought you were a kind, sensible girl."

Nuala flushed and looked obstinate.

"I don't want a stepmother," she said. "Only my father and Gran. She would spoil everything."

"Don't you trust your father?" continued the ballad singer. "And don't you trust your grandmother either? Do you think they would let anyone, anyone at all, treat you badly?"

"Want to go home!" wailed Danny.

"Me too!" roared his young brother. "Want Grannie!"

They began to weep, rubbing their faces until, between tears and dirt, they looked so queer that Séamus Rafferty laughed. He shook his head.

"I wish your uncle and aunt were home," he muttered. "Ah well, what can I do? I'd best be moving on. I've plans to get to another place by tonight."

He stood up and strapped his bundle on his back.

"Please stay with us till they come back," pleaded Garry. "They can't be so long now."

Séamus Rafferty grasped his stick firmly.

"No, I must be on my way! But you stay here and everything will be settled. Your aunt and uncle will take you home. You'll see, Nuala, things will work out all right. Nobody will blame you for making a mistake. Take my word for it."

He went off, swinging his stick and humming a song.

"You won't stand out against them, not if they want us to go home, not against Aunt Maureen, will you, Nuala?" asked Garry anxiously. "You couldn't stand against her."

Nuala stood staring at her brother.

"You're against me too!" she burst out. "Why didn't you let me go alone? Now you've spoiled everything! I don't want to go home! I won't stay with you! I'll go away by myself!"

She swung round furiously and ran off, speeding down the road. Danny and Peter looked at one another, caught hands and started to trot the way their sister had gone.

Garry pulled them back.

"Don't you start!" he said sternly. "We're going to stay here until Aunt Maureen and Uncle Des come home. That's the only thing I am sure of. We can't be running over the country, not knowing where we're going or where anyone else is. When they do come home they'll know what to do. Give us something to eat and drink and most likely take us back to Gran!"

"Hungry!" said Danny.

Peter frowned. He was thinking hard.

"Thirsty!" he said at last.

Garry had to laugh. He climbed to the top of the bank.

"If only Aunt Maureen and Uncle Des would come up that road and Nuala up the other one I wouldn't care for anything. But we can't just sit here. What shall I do?"

He jumped down.

"Come on, lads!" he said, trying to speak cheerfully. "I'm going to get into the house somehow. You watch and you'll see wonders."

He scrambled over the gate and pulled Peter and Danny after him. He strode towards the house, his brothers trying to keep up. Once more he tried the doors—back door, front door—both were locked. He tried the windows. They too were securely fastened.

"Upstairs!" said Danny, pointing. "Look!"

Garry looked.

The little window at the top of the stairs was ajar. Garry was sure he had looked at it before. But maybe he hadn't.

"It's so narrow," he pondered. "I suppose I just thought nobody could get in there. And Uncle Des could never dream it was possible. But perhaps it is."

A strong tree grew close to the back of the house.

"If I climb up there and take Peter with me. He's such a skinny little scrap I might be able to poke him through. But is he big enough to open the front door when he does get in?"

He stared at his young brother.

Peter smiled at him.

"Do you want to help me?" asked Garry.

Peter nodded.

"We're going to climb that tree," his big brother told him. "I'll go up first and I'll pull you up. Do exactly as I tell you and we'll be indoors in next to no time. Come along now."

Leaving his coat on the grass, Garry swung himself to the first branch, stood on it and stared at the wall so close to him. There was no sill to the narrow window and, when he stood on his toes, only the tips of his fingers could touch the bottom.

"What on earth am I to do?" he puzzled.

He looked down at the two little boys who were watching him, half anxious, half admiring. Their mouths opened in amazement as he climbed still higher, past the window. Their solemn little faces broke into smiles as he reached down, poked in his fingers, lifted the latch of the window so that it swung wide.

"Now we are getting somewhere!" he said cheerfully. "And I do believe I can squeeze through!

No need to bring young Peter into it!"

Clinging to the window frame he managed to force himself through. Still holding on he slipped down until his feet rested on the stairs. With a sigh of relief he let go and stood leaning against the banisters.

"That's the hardest part," he told himself. "Now the worst of our troubles are over."

But his spirits sank when he thought of Nuala.

"I do wish she was with us," he muttered. "Wonder what she's up to now?"

He opened the front door and called: "Come on, lads! Everything's O.K.!"

Danny and Peter heard him, but they were still gazing at the narrow window through which their brother had disappeared. When there was no sign of him they looked anxiously at one another. Their chubby little faces were screwed up and there were tears in the corners of their eyes when Garry appeared, looking as worried as they were.

"Thought you'd gone off, you young eejits!" he exclaimed. "Come on! I've the front door open!"

Peter's eyes danced.

"Nuala come back?" he asked eagerly.

"No, she hasn't!" Garry answered. "I do so wish she had. Why couldn't she have stayed with us?"

Like Grannie Brophy, Aunt Maureen tidied up after every meal, washed the crocks and laid the table again. The kettle, filled with fresh spring water, was standing clean and shining on the hearth, not too near the turf fire which still had a red glow.

Even on the hottest day Garry liked the cosy look of a fire.

"It's almost like home," he said, smiling at his brothers.

They smiled back and settled down comfortably on the hearthrug.

"Where's Jimsy?" asked Peter.

Jimsy was the Devlins' little dog. He had a black curly coat and four black paws. He was an important member of the family, for he had won prize after prize for his handsome appearance and he was a wonderful watch-dog.

They had taught Jimsy all kinds of tricks. But he would not stay in the house alone. Garry explained this but Peter wasn't satisfied. So they searched the sheds. Jimsy was not there.

"Hungry!" said Danny plaintively.

Garry laughed.

"There won't be much trouble about that," he said, opening the door of the larder which was beside the kitchen window.

"How about soda bread and blackberry jam?" he asked, looking at the shelves. "Here's a bottle of milk, but maybe that's wanted for tea. Here's some lemonade—a jug full. You know how good Aunt Maureen's lemonade is! And she said we could always help ourselves if we came and she wasn't in."

"Picnic!" cried Danny hopefully.

Garry knew what that meant—sitting on the

floor and drinking out of cups without saucers, not bothering about plates or making crumbs!

Danny and Peter were seated on the rug. Their big brother spread an old newspaper before them and laid out the provisions. He brought out a tin of ginger biscuits, the jug of lemonade, three cups and three red apples.

"Is this a party?" asked Danny, smiling happily.

"It's a picnic!" Garry told him. "People have to be invited to a party and nobody knows we're here. Don't eat too much and don't make crumbs."

"It is a party!" declared Danny. "Don't have biscuits for picnics."

"Have it your own way," chuckled Garry. "Only don't forget! We weren't asked. When Aunt Maureen and Uncle Des come, show your best manners and don't behave like a pair of travellers. Mind now!"

The two boys nodded.

They ate everything they could, including blackberry jam on the biscuits. When they were no longer hungry Peter yawned and they both nodded sleepily.

Garry found a face flannel, soaked it under the tap and wiped Danny's face and hands. A towel was hanging by the sink but he didn't see it, so he used the wiping-up cloth. It was clean and dry but rough. The little boy had grown too sleepy to notice.

"Wish Nuala was here," he thought. "She'd do this job better than me."

By the time Garry had finished with Danny, Peter had fallen asleep, his head against the front of the armchair, his legs stretched before him.

"Seems a pity to wake him," murmured Garry, "but I'll have to tidy him up before Aunt Maureen arrives."

So he washed their hands and faces and combed their hair. After that he made himself look smart and tidy. He felt much better when he had removed the dust of the journey.

"If only Nuala were here, this would be great fun," he thought. "I wonder where she is and what she is doing? Hey, who's this coming? Three cheers! It's Aunt Maureen and Uncle Des. They'll know what to do!"

He heard the key grate in the lock and rushed to the door.

15

With the Travellers

The travellers' caravan was jogging along the road, in shadow under the trees, in sunshine on the open road. They had a good stock of food at the back of the cart, including a sack of potatoes and a pound packet of tea. The baby had cut a new tooth without any bother at all and was sleeping peacefully.

"A good baby!" chuckled its father. "Never a word of complaint—when it's asleep! Isn't that right, Maggie?"

"None better!" agreed the mother, who was half asleep herself. "No more trouble than Wanderer."

Wanderer was the mare who had never strayed in her life.

"Please stop! Stop!" came a shout from behind them, followed by a tip-tapping of small feet trying to catch up.

"We want no strangers asking questions, wanting lifts," said Tomás severely. "Haven't we enough worries of our own?"

Maggie leaned round the side of the cart, shading

her eyes from the sun.

"That's no stranger! 'Tis that little gerrul we met with, up along. There were three young lads with her then. She's alone now."

"Take no notice of her," advised Tomás. "You'd never know what divilment them ones would be up to. Filled with consait if they're a scrap on the pretty side, and ready to fly off the handle if the world doesn't see eye to eye wid them. Ye were that way yerself when I got me first sight of ye."

Maggie tossed her head.

"Sure, we all have notions when we're that young," she said, laughing. "Ye had them yerself, if I remember rightly, an' ye were a good few years older than that poor child."

"She's catching up wid us," muttered Tomás. "Will I give her a clout and send her flying?"

"Leave the child alone," his wife told him indignantly. "Most likely she's in trouble at home. Listen to her story and do what we can to help."

"Have it yer own way," said Tomás comfortably.

"But I'm not taking on any more young runaways. Ye can't trust them. That sort will spin all kinds of yarns and we'd look grand if we were had up for kidnapping. We'd be the laugh of the whole countryside. Well, here she is."

"Will you give me a lift, please?" called a tearful voice.

Maggie looked down at Nuala.

"Here ye are again!" she called. "Give me yer hand, take a hold of the side there and jump.

That's the gerrul!"

Nuala landed on her hands and knees at Maggie's feet.

"I'm awful sorry to bother you!" she gasped. "If you could only just let me ride as far as the crossroads."

"Which ones?" asked Maggie. "The whole country's full of crossroads. There, there! Don't start crying again. Sit up here beside me and hold the babby. Are ye any good wid babbies?"

"I love them!" declared Nuala.

She sat in the corner of the seat. Maggie put the baby gently in her arms.

"The dote!" smiled Nuala.

The baby opened its dark eyes and looked up at Nuala very solemnly.

"Ah! Ah!" it gurgled, putting its thumb back in its mouth and closing its eyes again.

Maggie scrambled over the seat and disappeared in the back of the caravan.

"What are yez up to now, ye lazy divil?" demanded Tomás, who was marching beside the horse, a switch under his arm.

"Oh," exclaimed Nuala. "I'm not doing anything!"

"'Tis the baste I'm talking to, not yerself!" he explained. "Sit aisy now and don't ye be tormenting yerself about anything at all! Whatever yer trouble, the missus'll see ye righted. That's the class of wumman she is. Can't ever mind her own business and leave others to mind theirs. Anyway, the babby seems to have taken a fancy to ye, an' that goes for both of us."

"Thank you," said Nuala, very meekly.

"Tomás!" called Maggie.

"Listening!" answered Tomás.

"Will we stop for a bite and sup, or will we keep on and manage as best we can?"

"Stop!" shouted Tomás. "The young gerrul isn't used to feasting on the march, and 'tis a woeful waste to be spilling good strong tay over ourselves. Here's a good pull up. Hold on now! The baste is going to shift sideways."

The mare swung round, the cart rocked and heaved. Tomás jumped down and freed the mare from the shafts. There they were in the shadow of the trees. A fire was kindled almost at the striking of a match, for there was plenty of brushwood on the ground. Maggie took a handful of tea and emptied it into the pot, washed three cups at the spring surging down over a rocky ledge and then prepared the meal.

Tomás stretched full length on the grass, the baby on a sack beside him. Nuala perched on another sack while Maggie poured tea, cut bread and butter and handed round a tin of condensed milk.

"Sugar and milk in one," she murmured, "and who could ask for better."

At home Nuala would have despised such tea. But now she drank it thankfully and found it delicious. She could not help wondering what the boys were doing.

"Perhaps I should have stayed," she reflected. "But Aunt Maureen and Uncle Des might be back by now—so they'll be all right."

"That's the way Tomás does be," chuckled Maggie. "Talks and argues away to himself like an old duck quacking! I've heard some quare talk out of him, I'm telling ye!"

"Never give heed to what that wumman does be saying," Tomás told her. "'Tis great gas, listening! But I never mind her, never!"

"'Twould be better if ye did!" retorted Maggie. "If I had my way 'tis in a dacent little house on a main road we'd be living this day."

"And be stuck in the one place all our lives," said Tomás. "We'd be seeing the same people day in and day out until we'd be sick and tired of the sight of them, and ye'd be quarrelin' and jeerin' till they'd rise up and drive us from the parish."

"There do be places now," continued Maggie, paying not the slightest heed to her husband, "where they give ye a great stretch of land as well as the garden, mind ye, to grow vegetables in, and here we are, stravagin' the roads day and night, summer and winter, wid never a bit to show for all our labour! And, mind ye, Tomás, we're not getting any younger!"

"Why would we?" asked Tomás. "And look at the babby rolling round, content and happy. He's not complainin', why should we? Besides, what would ye do wid the bit of land and the garden?

Ye wouldn't know one end of a parsnip from the other if it was growing there before yer two eyes."

"Me grannie grows lovely parsnips," interrupted Nuala. "Me father says he'll send them in to the next flower show, so that she can win a prize."

Maggie poked a huge piece of bread and cheese into her mouth. Nuala wondered how she could manage such a mouthful. But in it went and she talked through it.

"Now wouldn't it be very quare for yer da to send parsnips in to a flower show!" exclaimed Maggie. "Sure, he must know they're not flowers, but more in the line of spuds and cabbage. Take a bite of bread and cheese, pet—'tis more filling than them biscuits."

"Don't be showing yer ignorance!" cried Tomás. "Ye'll have the young gerrul going back home giving them all a laugh when she tells them how the travelling people don't know flowers and veges are shown all at the one place. A nice show we'll be then! If we pass through the place they'll all be peeping through their windas to look at the ones that don't know parsnips from sunflowers, or cabbages from roses."

"I wonder do they argue like this all the time," thought Nuala. "Oh, I do wish I was home!"

She gazed along the road. Almost out of sight was a signpost. There were only two arms. On one was painted *Castle Moat.* The other read *Craigcullen.*

"If I run back now, maybe, Aunt Maureen and Uncle Des would be home. I know Garry won't jeer at me for changing my mind. If Aunt Maureen and Uncle Des aren't back it will be better still, for then no one will ever know I went off with the travellers. I'll wait till they're busy getting ready to start. Then I needn't explain and they won't mind. I expect they'll be really glad to be without me!"

"Eat up now!" urged Maggie. "There's an apple cake to folly. A dacent wumman over at Carrick gave it to me. She'd been throwing a party and the folks liked her sausage rolls so much they had no room left for the apple cake."

"'Twouldn't have hurt her to give ye a few of the rolls," grumbled Tomás.

"Sure, amn't I tellin' ye—they were all ate up!" protested his wife. "Ah, me lad, if we could only get one of them little houses, wid the gardens back and front, a gas stove, and 'lectric lighting in all the rooms, ye'd have nothing left to ax for. Why wouldn't ye put our names down for one? Then we would be made up!"

"They'd never give it to travellin' people!" said Tomás firmly. "Ye know that as well as I do. Besides, aren't we better off than the people living in them old rookeries that's falling down on top of 'em? I can tell you, they'd think themselves lucky to have a snug caravan like ours, not to mind the baste that's pulling it. Old Wanderer is a vallable bit of property, let me tell ye!"

Maggie was at her third cup of tea, feeling very comfortable and content. But she loved to continue the argument.

"Poor old Wanderer!" she said. "That mare would fetch enough to buy furniture and fixin's. 'Pon me word I don't know what has us stravagin' the roads in all kinds of weather, mostly bad, when we might be sittin' at our own fireside, wid a shelf of books over it and framed pictures on the walls."

"Ye're dotin'!" muttered Tomás. "Ye couldn't read the books if we had em!"

Nuala was staring at a clump of fir trees, with bluebells thick about their trunks. But she did not see them. What she did see was the sitting-room at home, Grannie Brophy in her armchair by the fire, the boys curled up on the sofa and their father sitting in his big chair at the table, turning over the pages of a new book from the village library.

She blinked for there was one missing from the group.

"I should be there," she thought resentfully. "There's room for me on the sofa!"

Maggie stood up, twisting her shawl about her shoulders.

"Time we were moving," she said.

Tomás fixed Wanderer's harness, swung Maggie up to the seat, handed her the baby and turned to Nuala.

"Well, girleen," he asked, "is it roving wid the travellers, or home to yer own people?"

Nuala made up her mind.

"Back to Castle Moat," she answered. "The boys are there and me aunt and uncle will stand by me. I'll tell them how kind you've been. Goodbye, and thank you very much."

"Wait a minit!" urged Tomás. "Now we're partin' and may never set eyes on one another again, tell us what made ye run away from home? Did yer mammy bate ye, or have ye been up to some mischief ye're afraid the father will find out?"

"I have no mammy," sighed Nuala. "But I have a lovely grandmother. She'd never beat me and I haven't been up to any mischief, only running away."

"Then what set ye goin'?" asked Maggie curiously.

Nuala bit her lip. She was determined not to cry. But it was very hard not to!

"'Tisn't any of their business," she thought, "but they have been kind."

She hung her head.

"Daddy's always going away on business," Nuala said slowly. "It's lovely when he comes home. He brings us sweets and presents. But this time he's bringing us a stepmother."

"A stepmother!" exclaimed Tomás, shaking his head.

Maggie shrugged her shoulders.

"There's stepmothers and stepmothers!" she exclaimed. "I had one and I wish she was with me now. We wouldn't be going the roads like this, I can tell ye. She was kindness itself. Go back and give the wumman a chance. You've done a foolish thing, but it's never too late to try again."

Nuala gasped with relief.

"Thank you," she murmured. "I'll go back to the boys and we'll go home together. I didn't think about people being different."

Away she went. She hadn't noticed the road they had come, so when it divided she kept to the left instead of the right and, before she realised what she had done, found herself on a path beside a swiftly flowing river.

The setting sun turned this to a stream of gold, but Nuala did not see its beauty.

"I'm wrong again!" she cried, stamping her foot. "How unlucky I am!"

She sat down on the trunk of a fallen tree. A branch poked up behind her and she leaned against it.

"I can go back the way I came," said Nuala to herself. "But if I do I may run into the travellers again and wouldn't I look silly! I don't believe Maggie would laugh at me but Tomás might. He'd look at me and shake his head."

She considered returning to the travellers.

"No!" she decided. "If I go back to them and Gran sent Garda Murphy in search of me, he might blame Tomás and Maggie for taking me away. That wouldn't be fair. I'll try to find out the right way to Castle Moat."

"I must go back to the boys," said Nuala out loud. "Maybe if I hurry I'll get there before Aunt Maureen and Uncle Des get home. Even if I don't they won't say anything—I know they won't."

Suddenly she longed, more than anything else,

to be back with Garry, with Danny, with Peter and her aunt and uncle. She wanted to be home with all of them, her grandmother and her father, even if it meant being with a stepmother.

"It can't be like it was in the legend," she reassured herself. "Nothing like that happens nowadays. The Children of Lir didn't have a grandmother to stand up for them, or an aunt and uncle. They didn't have a teacher like Miss Florrie."

She stood up quickly, swung round, slipped on the steep bank and went sliding down to the river. Too frightened even to scream, she flung out her arms. Her fingers clutched the low-growing branches of a rowan tree. She gripped tightly and lay still. Slowly, breathlessly, she moved over, so that she could hold the branches with both hands. She wasn't very heavy and she was able to pull herself through the water, closer to the tree. She crawled round its trunk, which was between her and the river, so that she would not slip again.

She looked at her hands. They were thick with wet clay. Her shoes were covered too, and her socks were plastered with mud while her frock was dirty and crumpled.

"I must be a terrible sight," she sighed in dismay. "Even the travellers would be ashamed to be seen with me now!"

16

Explanations

Before Uncle Des could turn the key in the lock of his front door it was flung open and there stood Garry, with the younger boys peeping out, one on each side.

"'Pon me word!" exclaimed Des Devlin, looking at them in amazement. "How in the wide world did you get in?"

Garry pulled his brothers away from the door as their aunt and uncle walked in.

Aunt Maureen looked at the children, then at her husband in a pleased but bewildered way.

"We heard from Gran Brophy that you had run away from home," she said, "but when you did not come here, we didn't know where to look for you."

Garry flushed as he tried to explain—without blaming Nuala—all that had happened.

"I know I shouldn't have climbed in the window but we were hungry and tired. We waited and we hoped you would come back soon, but it seemed a terrible long time. I hope you're not cross."

"We aren't cross at all," declared his aunt. "We're very glad to see you. But you must promise you won't do it again. You might have fallen from the tree and injured yourself. But where is Nuala? Why isn't she with you? I thought you said it was she who wanted to run away. But why?"

By this time they were all inside. Aunt Maureen and Uncle Des had settled themselves in the big armchairs, the boys curled up on the sofa.

Garry frowned. "Nuala went off. She may be home now. Didn't you have a letter from Dad?" he added.

"We did!" said his uncle.

Aunt Maureen looked from one serious young face to the others.

"Did he tell you about the stepmother he's bringing home?" asked the boy.

"So that's it!" exclaimed Uncle Des. "I wondered how your grannie would take it. I never dreamed that you children would be upset."

"What a home-coming for that poor girl!" said Aunt Maureen. And Garry knew she wasn't thinking of Nuala.

Uncle Des was going out the door when Aunt Maureen called him back.

"I think you'd better ask Sergeant O'Gorman to bring the car and take us all over to Craigcullen. Grannie Brophy doesn't know where any of the children are. The sooner she sees the boys and hears about Nuala the better she'll be pleased."

"You're right, dead right!" agreed Uncle Des.

"Into your coats, lads, and be ready. It won't take them long to get the car out." He hurried away.

Soon the big black Garda car was surging down the road and stopped in front of the house with a grinding of brakes. There was plenty of room for them all. Garry didn't know whether he should feel proud or ashamed of being taken home by Garda in uniform. But he stretched his legs in front of him just as they did and tried to look big and important.

"People might think we're being arrested for thieving or house-breaking," he thought. "Only there won't be anyone to see what we're doing. Wish we lived in the village—then there would be a fuss."

He was too confused and excited to notice which way they went. But there they were, slowing down at the cottage. The door was flung open and the children's grandmother stood staring at the car.

Grannie Brophy backed away from the door, putting her hand over her mouth to keep herself from crying out. She saw Aunt Maureen standing up while the boys jumped down and ran towards her.

"Thank God you're safe!" she cried, trying to hug the three of them all at once. "But where is Nuala?"

Sergeant O'Gorman jumped down and strode across.

"Has anything happened to the child—anything

bad?" she whispered.

"Not at all! Not at all, ma'am!" said the sergeant soothingly. "We've brought the boys back, and Mr and Mrs Devlin came along to see how we can find the little girl as soon as possible. We think no harm can have come to her. You'd be surprised how quickly we hear the bad news. And when there's no bad news, we can hope that any news will be good."

He smiled down at her.

"Hadn't we as well go inside and talk it over? The sooner I know the whole story, the sooner we'll know where to go looking for the young girl."

Mrs Brophy looked confused.

"I'm sorry, terrible sorry!" she stammered. "You must forgive me. I'm so mixed up I don't know am I on me head or me heels! Come in, all of you, and sit down. Take the armchair and make yourself at home, sergeant. Maureen, if you'd put on the kettle we'd decide what's best to be done. Wouldn't it be as well, sergeant, if the other young man came inside? He might be a great help, for he knows everyone in these parts as well as I do. A cup of tea would be good for us all and the poor children must be starving!"

"I could do with a spot of tea!" agreed the sergeant heartily, lowering himself carefully into the big armchair, which he filled. "Now—the whole story!"

Gran Brophy nodded.

"And the beginning is—why did the children run away? You tell that, Garry."

Garry frowned.

"Be a good, sensible lad," pleaded his grandmother. "You must know something of what has happened. You tell us that—it may help the sergeant to find Nuala."

"It was all because of Dad bringing home a new mother," began the boy. "Nuala was thinking about the story you told us—the four Swan Children. She thought that all stepmothers were wicked and cruel!"

He paused, feeling puzzled. The sergeant was impatient.

"Hurry, lad—we can't sit here all night! Tell us where the girleen meant to go. Remember, she's out there in the rain."

"To Aunt Maureen and Uncle Des, of course," Garry told him. "We tried to go by the shore road but the sea was all over it. So we went across the bog. We went to sleep in a turf hut and in the morning we took a lift on a turf cart—"

"Ye took a lift on a turf cart," the sergeant interrupted. "Now what do ye mean by that!"

"There was no one with it," explained the boy. "We were tired, so we climbed into the cart and went to sleep until we got to Carragh which is near Sligo. I think it was Sligo because that was the name over the post office. You see we usually go to Bundoran."

"Fair enough!" agreed the sergeant. "But ye

must have been nigh starving by this time! I know what young lads are."

Garry glanced guiltily at his grandmother.

"We did take some biscuits and cheese, and a box of dates and a lump of seed cake."

"Thanks be for that!" the old woman exclaimed.

"Keep on!" interrupted the big man in the armchair. "We've still to find young Nuala!"

They had begun to feel drowsy. But what the sergeant said jerked them to attention. The wind, heavy with rain, was beating against the window. The thought of Nuala alone out in the storm, made them anxious.

"Ye reached Sligo!" snapped the sergeant. "Then what?"

Garry nodded.

"We jumped out of the cart and ran as fast as we could. We bought some apples. Then we got a lift with some travellers. They brought us to Castle Moat."

"Fair enough!" murmured the big man again. "Ye came to yer uncle's place. But what happened the little girl?"

Garry shook his head.

"She got into a temper because I wanted to come back home and she ran off. She went down the road the travellers took. Maybe she's with them now."

"Travellers!" exclaimed Gran Brophy. "Me poor little Nuala with travellers!"

"D'ye know the names that's on them?" asked

Sergeant O'Gorman.

"I do!" answered the boy. "They're Maggie and Tomás O'Driscoll.

"Then she's safe enough," declared the sergerant. "They're a decent pair, who'll do their best for the child. I wouldn't be the least bit surprised if they didn't coax her to stay with them till they can get her back home."

Everyone looked at him with admiring eyes. They felt that if all their troubles weren't already settled, they soon would be.

The sergeant stood up.

"We'll be off after those travellers," he said. "I make no promises, but if I don't come back with the child this very night I'll—I'll—!"

He paused.

"Eat yer cap!" suggested his fellow Garda helpfully.

Sergeant O'Gorman gave him such a scornful look that Aunt Maureen, who had been pouring out the tea, hurriedly handed the sergeant a big cup, brimful, and then held out a plate of buttered soda bread.

He refused the soda bread, drank the hot tea at one gulp and stood up.

"Stir yer stumps, lad!" the sergeant ordered the young Garda. "Remember, we've still to find the child!"

The young man sprang to his feet and was out of the door while Aunt Maureen was thrusting a cup of tea towards him.

"Ye don't want to go making a pet of that boyo!" the sergeant told her. "He'd settle down here with that fine cat and think he'd done his duty by all. Goodbye now and we'll have news for you before the night's out. I can promise that."

They watched him striding down the path. As the garden gate swung behind him Uncle Des rubbed his hands.

"I'm thinking we'll see little Nuala back safe and sound before long. That's a good man."

Grannie Brophy sighed.

"If only she comes before her father and that poor girl he's bringing with him. If only he'd prepared us! 'Twould have given me a chance and I'd never have told that sad story."

"If the sergeant does bring Nuala back before Tim and the girl arrive it will be all right," said Aunt Maureen. "There'll be too much to talk about, too much excitement for them to discover what's been happening here."

She looked round hopefully.

"I won't say a word," promised Garry. "And you can trust Nuala."

"How about the young lads?" asked Uncle Des. His wife laughed.

"Even if they talk, who is going to understand a word they say? Have sense, man, do!"

"Maybe if *we* stop talking, they'll forget all about it!" suggested the grandmother.

"When's Nuala coming home?" asked Danny.

"Want my Nuala!" said Peter.

"Drink your milk like good boys and then you can go to bed," she told them.

"Want a story first," insisted Danny. "A nice, long, funny story!"

"Want Nuala!" said Peter grumblingly.

"I feel I'll never venture to tell a story again," said the grandmother. "If only I'd told any other story in the world last time!"

"Let's sing a song!" suggested Garry. "How about that one you sang the time I hurt my leg and I had to lie with it stretched out. We never learned it properly. I got well too soon. Let's try now! You begin, Gran!"

The grandmother pushed away her empty tea cup. She had a sweet, clear voice and she knew more songs even that Uncle Des, who was always winning prizes for singing at the Feis competitions. But she had no heart for singing this night. She knew her manners and smiled over at Uncle Des.

Uncle Des loved singing songs with a rousing refrain. He started at once before Aunt Maureen could stop him.

"Come! Pull up to the fire
And I'll sing ye a song—
A song with a chorus,
That won't be too long;
Sure it won't be too long!"

Everybody joined in and sang,

"Sure, it won't be too long!
Tis a song I heard sung
A long, long time ago,
When I was a young lad
Away in Mayo!
Living down in Mayo!

'Twas young Paudeen sang it—
A wild song of the sea;
Of pirates, and shipwrecks,
Bold, careless and free.
Bold, careless and free!

There was shouting and fighting,
Music and dancing,
Eating and drinking,
Cavorting and prancing!
Cavorting and prancing!"

"Listen!" interrupted Aunt Maureen, putting her head on one side. "What's that noise?"

They all sat silent as the sound of a car driving along the road came to them. They heard three hoots of a horn.

"Mercy on us!" exclaimed Grannie Brophy. "'Tis Himself, and no doubt he has Herself with him!"

She slipped over to the door and flung it wide.

"Come in and welcome!" she called.

But her voice was quavering.

"God bless us!" murmured Des Devlin. "It just could be Tim and his bride!"

17

The Search

Firelight and lamplight streamed out through the darkness. For the first time in his life Garry did not rush to greet his father. The little boys squeezed closer together, while Boots stood up, his ears twitching, his bushy tail waving like a fan.

Uncle Des and Aunt Maureen smiled at each other and moved just behind Grannie Brophy, so that the two travellers saw a group of friendly faces as they blinked their way in.

"I've brought you a new daughter," said Tim Brophy to his mother. "But I've written you all about her. You know her name—Eva."

For a moment they all stood staring in silence at the young woman who came in through the lighted doorway.

"A real beauty," thought Uncle Des admiringly.

"What a kind face," said his wife to herself, and her own face had a smile of welcome.

"Here's me sister Maureen and her husband Des—I've told you all about them," stammered Tim Brophy, so excited he could hardly speak.

"How good of you to be here to meet me," said the stranger in a soft low voice, which made Peter and Danny want to be friends with her.

She bent down to kiss Grannie Brophy. As she stood up Aunt Maureen flung her arms round her.

"If that brother of mine isn't a lucky fellow!" she exclaimed. "And here's me husband, Des Devlin, as delighted to meet you as I am myself, Eva!"

"And you are surely Garry, the big boy of the family," said the newcomer, her soft lips touching the boy's cheek. "I do hope we'll be great friends in the days before us. But where is Nuala, the wonderful little girl I've been hearing so much about?"

With her hand on Garry's shoulder she turned to the old woman, her big soft brown eyes wandering about the room.

"The child isn't sick, is she?" asked Tim Brophy anxiously. "She seemed grand when I went away."

For a moment the room was silent, except for a patter-patter as a few scraps of turf dropped out on the hearth. Gran Brophy opened her mouth to speak but could not. Garry clapped her thin hand in his strong warm one.

"Nuala isn't sick," he said firmly. "She just went off after the travellers!"

He told the story in a rush of words.

"We crossed over the bog to go to Aunt Maureen's and we got into a turf cart. We fell asleep and it took us to Sligo instead. So it was ages before we did get to Castle Moat. The house was locked up because Uncle Des and Aunt Maureen were at the fair. We managed to get in and, when they came back, they brought us here."

His father stared at him.

"I can see you're safe and sound," he burst out, "but where is your sister?"

Garry flushed.

"She got into a temper and ran off after Maggie and Tomás—they're the travellers!"

The others were silent but Tim spoke.

"Run off after the travellers! Are you crazy? What could send a daughter of mind chasing after the likes of them?"

He turned to his mother.

"What is this nonsense?" he said. "Can you explain?"

The old woman looked at the young one—the stranger—and sighed.

"'Tis all my fault," she said. "Most nights I tell the children a story before they go to bed, and just before this happened I told them the story of the Children of Lir."

Eva smiled, though she looked puzzled.

"The Swan Children!" exclaimed Tim Brophy. "That's a grand story—one of the best!" He looked at his mother and shrugged his shoulders.

She nodded.

"'Tis a lovely story though a sad one, and if I'd known you were bringing this dear girl home to us, I'd not have chosen to tell them that story. It was foolish but how was I to know?"

Eva nodded. By this time they were all seated.

"Listen, Garry!" said his father. "You tell me what happened right from the beginning."

The boy rubbed his chin.

"It was this way, Dad! When we went up to bed I wasn't sleepy, so I stood at the window looking out. I could see four white swans on the bay. I wouldn't have noticed them only for the story we'd heard. I was wondering about this, wishing I knew who first told it, when I heard a noise downstairs."

"Go on!" ordered his father. "And don't be too long. I want Nuala back here as soon as possible."

"I came down," continued the boy, "and there was Nuala packing her school bag with biscuits and all kinds of things to eat. She said she wasn't going to stay here if Daddy was going to bring home a stepmother."

He paused and looked apologetically at Eva.

"If only she'd waited," he said, "but she really was scared. I thought if I went with her it mightn't be so bad. Then the two young ones came down and we had to take them. Of course they didn't understand. They thought we were just going out for a lark."

"Go on!" snapped Tim Brophy. "I would have thought you'd have a little more sense. After all, you're the eldest."

"Nuala is very gentle," said the grandmother, "but she can be very obstinate." She looked pleadingly at her son.

"We didn't mean to run away, not really," said the boy quickly. "Only to go to Aunt Maureen and Uncle Des! Nuala thought they'd stand by us."

Uncle Des smiled and shook his head.

"There's this excuse for that little noodle!" he exclaimed. "She hadn't seen her stepmother!"

"Go on! Go on, for pity's sake!" said Tim.

"The tide was desperate high. That was why we took the bog road," continued Garry. "It was very dark and those young ones were terrible slow. We found the turf-cutters' hut and we went to sleep there. In the morning we took some of the coffee and food the men had left. They came along and we hid in their cart.

"We thought they'd be taking the turf to Castle Moat and we'd be with Aunt Maureen before Gran missed us. Instead we came to Sligo. We managed to get out of the cart before the men could stop us. Then we did set off for Castle Moat."

He stopped, unable to say another word. Eyes seemed to be staring at him whichever way he looked. He knew if he couldn't get out of the room he'd burst into tears. Already he felt ashamed. He pushed past his father and rushed out of the cottage, down the path.

At the crossroads close by, he caught sight of the black shiny Garda car which had been cruising round trying to find some trace of Nuala or the travellers. The two men were standing by it, considering which way to go next. He scrambled inside and crouched down at the back. Neither of the men noticed him.

"The young fool!" muttered Tim Brophy. "I'd best go after him! It's bad enough to lose one child without missing the other! Come along, Des!"

"We can separate and find Nuala quicker," said Tim to his mother over his shoulder. "I won't be away long! You look after Herself!"

He smiled at Eva. Then he and Des hurried out.

The sergeant jumped into the Garda car, just missing standing on Garry, who made himself as small as he could.

"Let you take the main road, we'll go in and out," called the sergeant to Tim Brophy, who had climbed into his own car. "Keep on hooting every hundred yards or so."

Down by the river Nuala, in the shelter of the rowan bush, tried to clean her muddy hands with bunches of wet grass. She took little notice of the motor horns hooting. This was only another noise added to the sounds of wind and rain, the roar of the river, the rustling of trees.

The light had faded from the sky. She could hear, but not see, the river. She started as a light flashed in her face, and crouched close to the ground as another flash followed.

Voices called: "Nuala! Nuala!"

Nuala heard nothing but the confused roar of wind and rushing water. She could not hear the voices that called her name and did not know her father was close by and seeking her.

The lights moved away. The sound of the horns died in the distance. Only the wind, tossing branches, and the rush of the river reached her. Soon came a heavier downpour of rain. In a few moments Nuala was soaked.

Shivering, she stumbled towards a dark shadowy mass and found herself in the shelter of trees. She pressed against a dry trunk and, feeling about, found a broad branch spreading near the ground. She sank down, wriggling in among the leaves.

She was weary. Leaves and the small twiggy branches made a resting-place. She could hear the rain but did not feel it now.

"If I could find the road maybe I'd come up with Maggie and Tomás," she thought. "I could ask them to take me home."

Nuala could hear the river surging towards the bridge. It made her feel sleepy and confused.

"I'll wait till the moon comes up and shows me the way," she decided.

Her eyes closed. Above her, on the road, her father drove slowly along, shouting "Nuala! Nuala!" and sounding his horn as he peered at the hedges.

"No luck!" he muttered in dismay. "Perhaps the Garda have better news. I'll go home! I don't want to leave Eva alone too long!"

He went slowly, hooting, calling "Nuala! Nuala!" The noise of the wind and rain drowned his voice and the sound of the horn. At last he was back at the house.

He sat hooting till Gran Brophy came to the

door.

"Any luck?" called Tim. "Has she come back?"

The old woman shook her head.

"Is Garry with you?" she asked.

Tim stared at her in amazement.

"With me!" he echoed. "Why should he be? I saw nothing of him."

They stood looking at each other.

"Thank God, the little fellows are safe," murmured Grannie Brophy.

While they stood there, not knowing what to do, Nuala was scrambling back to the road. The rain was still falling, but she kept in the shelter of the hedge. Luckily there were no ditches and the moon was now shining.

She came to a signpost but could not see the names on it.

"I think I'd best keep straight on," she decided. But she did not move, for through the darkness she thought she saw the glow of a camp fire, with its promise of warmth and companionship. Could this be where Maggie and Tomás had halted for the night?

She hurried on and there they were.

How cosy their camp looked. She couldn't see the baby, for it was sound asleep in a snug nest of old coats. But the van had been drawn up on a rocky patch, under thick overhanging trees, where not a drop of rain could disturb their blazing fire.

Two shawls were spread on the ground. A sack was hung against the side of the van. Tomás was building up the fire with short, thick, dry branches, while Maggie stirred a pot of stew with a big iron spoon.

"Rest aisy now!" she said. "The fire's grand and the stew needs only another stir or two before we can settle down to it. Push over the kettle and that dish there, draw it away from the flames. 'Tis a grand lump of pudden and I wouldn't want it burned."

Tomás lifted his head and peered into the darkness.

"What ails ye now?" asked Maggie. "I never knew such a one! Can't ye ever rest aisy?"

"Not when there's strangers spying on us! Hi there! Come into the light, whoever ye are! Come on! Show yerself or I'll aim a burning brand at yer head!"

"Don't! Don't!" cried Nuala in terror. "It's me! Nuala Brophy!"

She stepped into the firelight, her hands held out appealingly.

"If this doesn't beat all!" exclaimed Tomás. "I'm beginning to think there's something quare about that young one."

Maggie stood back from the fire, shading her eyes.

"What ails ye now, pet?" she asked. "Come over to the fire and let's hear all about it. Take off that wet heavy coat and hang it on the branch yonder. Sit there on the log. The stew's ready to lift. Tip the paper of tay into the can, Tomás, and we'll be fixed. We've sugar to spare, not to mind the bottle of milk."

"Isn't that for the babby?" grumbled Tomás.

"Sure, the little fella wouldn't grudge us the drop for a sup of tay," Maggie told him.

Nuala stepped cautiously over to the log. She settled back, leaning against the cart. Almost at once there was a tin bowl of stew in her hands, a spoon standing upright in it. The smell of hot meat, onions, potatoes, thyme, rose up and, without questions or explanations, the three of them were eating away.

"I didn't know I was so hungry," murmured Nuala. "It's lovely stew, almost as good as Gran's."

"Almost!" cried Tomás indignantly.

"Whisht!" said Maggie peaceably. "Don't ye understand that's the biggest praise the child can give?"

And there they sat spooning up stew until the baby woke and cried for his share.

At once his mother was beside him, a spoonful of bread soaked in the thick hot gravy held to his lips.

"Isn't he the great little guzzler?" said his father admiringly.

When the billy can of tea was drawn away from the fire, milk and sugar put into two enamel cups, and a tin mug for the visitor, Tomás became curious again.

He put his elbows on his knees, peered through the smoke rising steadily between them and pushed back his old caubeen.

"Now, young one, the whole story," he demanded. "Ye owe us that. Then we can see what's to be done."

Nuala's mouth was filled with hot, well-buttered soda bread. She was holding up the tin mug of good strong sweet tea.

She looked at Maggie.

"Will ye let the child finish with her aitin' an drinkin'!" cried Maggie. "Sure, even if we are travellers, we can still behave like civilised human creatures!"

"Have it yer own way!" muttered Tomás, swallowing a mouthful of tea. "But when we're put in jail for life, and our young one taken from us, don't blame me! Mind, I'm telling ye!"

"Ah, God be good to me!" gasped Maggie. "Why would that be happening to us? Tell me that now?"

Her husband glared across the fire at her.

"For kidnapping!" he snapped. "Did ye never hear tell of that?"

Maggie put down her mug of tea.

"Sure, we're not kidnapping the young gerrul! She's as free to come and go as we are. And if her people get all het up because she's run from them, is it our fault? Why don't they look after her better?"

Tomás held up his hand.

"Will ye stop blathering for one small minit, wumman. Listen now! Tell me what ye hear?

Listen, do!"

Maggie listened. So did Nuala.

Far away, yet drawing nearer **every** moment, came the tooting of a horn—One! One—two! One—two—three!

"'Tis the Garda! Bad scran to them!" muttered Tomás.

"Ah, don't make me tired!" protested Maggie. "Aren't they only trying to find the child? Doing their duty! Isn't that what we pay them for?"

Tomás looked at her and shook his head.

"I like that! What *we* pay them for! How are ye! They'd grow fat on what they get out of the likes of us!"

Maggie looked over at Nuala.

"Do ye want to stay with us, child, or will ye go back home? Remember this—if ye're happy with yer young stepmother ye need never give a look at us if we meet! Make up yer mind. Will ye give her a try? Or will we keep quiet in this snug corner? But—mind now—there's yer grannie an yer da to think of!"

Nuala sprang to her feet and snatched up her coat.

"I'll go back," she said firmly. "I've been a coward and I've upset everybody. Thank you for all your kindness! Goodbye!"

She ran off down the road.

"Go along and keep and eye on her!" snapped Maggie. "Tomás, will ye get a move on! Don't come back until you're sure she's safe."

She gave her husband, who was rising slowly, a push that almost sent him into the fire.

"'Pon me word!" he exclaimed. "Ye have me nearly murdered, wumman!"

"Get along, do!" retorted Maggie.

He went away from the fire, slowly at first, then quicker and quicker until he was running. He caught up with Nuala as she reached the crossroads and took her hand.

"Don't be afeard!" he told her. "I'll see ye righted!"

"Hi there!" he shouted. "Hi, Garda! Are ye looking for a lost young gerrul? I have her here, safe and sound!"

The light of a powerful headlamp missed Nuala but caught Tomás as he stepped in front of her.

The Garda car was standing by the signpost. Sergeant O'Gorman leaped to the road with Garda Cassidy following so closely he nearly sent his superior officer flying. Both were so absorbed in what they saw that they held on to each other in silence and stared as Nuala stepped towards thems.

"Where did ye find her?" demanded the sergeant at last. "And who are ye? Speak up, man!"

18

An End and a Beginning

There was Nuala, sitting up in the car beside Sergeant O'Gorman. She answered every question he asked until she felt she couldn't answer another single one.

"Ah well," he said, "we have ye safe. Ye won't be so foolish again, will ye, girleen? Promise!"

"I promise," murmured Nuala.

A hand reached up from the floor of the car and squeezed hers.

"Oh!" she exclaimed. "Oh!"

"What's that?" demanded the sergeant. "Did I push you?"

Nuala shook her head.

"It's me!" announced Garry, kneeling up beside his sister, "I came along to help find Nuala!"

"Ye did, did ye!" said Sergeant O'Gorman. "'Pon me word, I'm beginning to pity that poor young woman. She doesn't know what she's taken on, unless yer dad had the sense to warn her. 'Tis a mercy there's yer grannie to stand by her."

"I'll never run away again whatever happens! Honest I won't!" declared Nuala.

"If ye do, I hope yer da takes a good stout stick to ye!" he said.

He spoke fiercely, and in the darkness Nuala couldn't see that he was grinning.

"I know I've been bold," she said indignantly. "But he'd never do that! Never!"

"If he had, me lassyo, he'd have saved himself, and the rest of us, a deal of trouble."

"Gran wouldn't let him!" declared Garry triumphantly. "And I don't believe the stepmother would either!"

Nuala looked at him in a puzzled way but said nothing.

"I was thinking of taking the pair of ye to the barracks and ringing up headquarters," the sergeant told them. "But if ye promise to behave yourselves, and not be tormenting yer family any more, I'll leave them to deal with ye. Do you promise?"

"I will!" said Garry.

"Me too!" murmured Nuala.

She leaned forward as they turned the corner and drove into the lighted path steaming out from the open door of the home.

"Did you find them?" asked a quavering voice as Grannie Brophy stepped forward, the others peering over her head.

"I did!" answered the sergeant. "Like sensible children they came quiet and promised to reform. So I didn't have to put the handcuffs on them.

Seems 'twas all a mistake. Give them a chance this time and I'm sure ye'll have no bother at all. Here they are! I'll bring them out to ye! Are the others back?"

Neither Nuala nor Garry knew how it happened, but in next to no time the whole Brophy family—including their new stepmother—were sitting round the fire, drinking tea and eating thick hot slices of well-buttered toast.

Nuala had eaten so much of the travellers' stew that she could only sip and nibble. The others, even Grannie Brophy, ate as if they were starving.

"Ah well," said Tim Brophy, "I've often heard it said that all's well that ends well, though 'twas a terrible home-coming for you, Eva! I don't suppose you'll ever forget it!"

Eva looked at him solemnly over her teacup, but her big dark eyes were twinkling.

"I don't believe I will," she told him. "And I don't know that I'll want to."

"The children should go to bed," murmured Grannie Brophy. "At least Danny and Peter should. Look, they're falling asleep!"

"Carry me," ordered Peter, yawning.

"I'll walk," mumbled Danny.

Yet when his father tucked him under one arm and Peter under the other, he made no effort to resist, but hung as limply as his brother.

"I'm not sleepy, not a bit," declared Garry.

"Nor me," whispered Nuala, trying not to blink. But when her father leaned back on the sofa, crossed his legs, folded his arms and looked sternly at her, she wished she could have followed her younger brothers.

"What came over you, Nuala?" he asked. "You're the last one I expected to behave in such a foolish way! And you too, Garry! A lad of your age!"

"Haven't I told you 'twas all my fault!" protested Grannie Brophy. "The children have gone through enough. Such a thing will never happen again. If there's any more story-telling to be done in this house I'll not be the one to do it!"

"Oh," exclaimed Eva, "I've been looking forward to your stories so much! Tim has told me all about them."

She gave Grannie a warm friendly smile.

"No one ever told me such stories until Tim came along," she continued, "and he said he had them all from you."

"I do know a few and that's the truth," murmured the grandmother. "But you'll be too busy making friends and finding yer way around to want to listen to me!"

"Oh no, I won't" said Eva firmly. "There'll be plenty of time for that!"

Upstairs Nuala, a big shawl wrapped round her, over her nightgown, looked out from her bedroom window.

The full moon flooded the bay with light, the waves thundered in, their foam-tipped crests glistening like silver lace. In the distance the lighthouse, gleaming like a new toy, flung its beams against the dark sky.

"Wish I could go out there!" thought Nuala, leaning forward eagerly.

Her eyes strayed to the towering mass of Ben Bulben, pushing its great shoulder through the mist. She thought of the legends her grandmother had told them of the heroes and ancient queens who wandered over the heights. On the other side was Knocknarea, half hidden by mist, pierced with shafts of silver moonlight.

"The Good People! They belong out there," she whispered. "I like them the best of all in the stories that Gran tells!"

She stood silent, her eyes startled and wondering, as up from the tossing waters of the bay soared four great white swans, one after the other in a wavering line, their glistening wings outspread, their long necks thrust forward. They flew on and vanished into the darkness beyond.

"Goodbye!" said Nuala softly. "I hope all your troubles are over, as mine are now."

Children's Poolbeg Books

Author	Title	ISBN	Price
Banville Vincent	*Hennessy*	1 85371 132 2	£3.99
Beckett Mary	*Orla was Six*	1 85371 047 4	£2.99
Beckett Mary	*Orla at School*	1 85371 157 8	£2.99
Comyns Michael	*The Trouble with Marrows*	1 85371 117 9	£2.99
Considine June	*When the Luvenders came to Merrick Town*	1 85371 055 5	£4.50
Considine June	*Luvenders at the Old Mill*	1 85371 115 2	£4.50
Considine June	*Island of Luvenders*	1 85371 149 7	£4.50
Corcoran Clodagh ed.	*Baker's Dozen*	1 85371 050 4	£3.50
Corcoran Clodagh ed.	*Discoveries*	1 85371 019 9	£4.99
Cruickshank Margrit	*SKUNK and the Ozone Conspiracy*	1 85371 067 9	£3.99
Cruickshank Margrit	*SKUNK and the Splitting Earth*	1 85371 119 5	£3.99
Daly Ita	*Candy on the DART*	1 85371 057 1	£2.99
Daly Ita	*Candy and Sharon Olé*	1 85371 159 4	£3.50
Dillon Eilís	*The Seekers*	1 85371 152 7	£3.50
Dillon Eilís	*The Singing Cave*	1 85371 153 5	£3.99
Duffy Robert	*Children's Quizbook No.1*	1 85371 020 2	£2.99
Duffy Robert	*Children's Quizbook No.2*	1 85371 052 0	£2.99
Duffy Robert	*Children's Quizbook No.3*	1 85371 099 7	£2.99
Duffy Robert	*The Euroquiz Book*	1 85371 151 9	£3.50
Ellis Brendan	*Santa and the King of Starless Nights*	1 85371 114 4	£2.99
Henning Ann	*The Connemara Whirlwind*	1 85371 079 2	£3.99
Henning Ann	*The Connemara Stallion*	1 85371 158 6	£3.99
Hickey Tony	*Blanketland*	1 85371 043 1	£2.99
Hickey Tony	*Foodland*	1 85371 075 X	£2.99
Hickey Tony	*Legendland*	1 85371 122 5	£3.50
Hickey Tony	*Where is Joe?*	1 85371 045 8	£3.99
Hickey Tony	*Joe in the Middle*	1 85371 021 0	£3.99
Hickey Tony	*Joe on Holiday*	1 85371 145 4	£3.50
Hickey Tony	*Spike & the Professor*	1 85371 039 3	£2.99
Hickey Tony	*Spike and the Professor and Doreen at the Races*	1 85371 089 X	£3.99
Hickey Tony	*Spike, the Professor and Doreen in London*	1 85371 130 6	£3.99
Kelly Eamon	*The Bridge of Feathers*	1 85371 053 9	£2.99
Lavin Mary	*A Likely Story*	1 85371 104 7	£2.99
Lynch Patricia	*Brogeen and the Green Shoes*	1 85371 051 2	£3.50
Lynch Patricia	*Brogeen follows the Magic Tune*	1 85371 022 9	£3.99
Lynch Patricia	*Sally from Cork*	1 85371 070 9	£3.99
Lynch Patricia	*The Turfcutter's Donkey*	1 85371 016 4	£3.99
MacMahon Bryan	*Patsy-O*	1 85371 036 9	£3.50
McCann Sean	*Growing Things*	1 85371 029 6	£2.99
McMahon Sean	*The Poolbeg Book of Children's Verse*	1 85371 080 6	£4.99
McMahon Sean	*Shoes and Ships and Sealing Wax*	1 85371 046 6	£2.99
McMahon Sean	*The Light on Illancrone*	1 85371 083 0	£3.50
McMahon Sean	*The Three Seals*	1 85371 148 9	£3.99
Mullen Michael	*The Viking Princess*	1 85371 015 6	£2.99
Mullen Michael	*The Caravan*	1 85371 074 1	£2.99
Mullen Michael	*The Little Drummer Boy*	1 85371 035 0	£2.99
Mullen Michael	*The Long March*	1 85371 109 8	£3.50
Mullen Michael	*The Flight of the Earls*	1 85371 146 2	£3.99
Ní Dhuibhne Eilís	*The Uncommon Cormorant*	1 85371 111 X	£2.99

Author	Title	ISBN	Price
Ní Dhuibhne Eilís	Hugo and the Sunshine Girl	1 85371 160 8	£3.50
Ó hEithir Breandán	An Nollaig Thiar	1 85371 044 X	£2.99
Ó Faoláin Eileen	The Little Black Hen	1 85371 049 0	£2.99
Ó Faoláin Eileen	Children of the Salmon	1 85371 003 2	£3.99
Ó Faoláin Eileen	Irish Sagas and Folk Tales	0 90516 971 9	£3.95
Quarton Marjorie	The Cow Watched the Battle	1 85371 084 9	£2.99
Quarton Marjorie	The Other Side of the Island	1 85371 161 6	£3.50
Quinn John	The Summer of Lily and Esme	1 85371 162 4	£3.99
Ross Gaby	Damien the Dragon	1 85371 078 4	£2.99
Schulman Anne	Children's Book of Puzzles	1 85371 133 0	£3.99
Snell Gordon	Cruncher Sparrow High Flier	1 85371 100 4	£2.99
Snell Gordon	Cruncher Sparrow's Flying School	1 85371 163 2	£2.99
Stanley-Higel Mary	Poolbeg Book of Children's Crosswords 1	1 85371 098 9	£2.99
Stanley-Higel Mary	Poolbeg Book of Children's Crosswords 2	1 85371 150 0	£3.50
Swift Carolyn	Bugsy Goes to Cork	1 85371 071 7	£3.50
Swift Carolyn	Bugsy Goes to Limerick	1 85371 014 8	£3.50
Swift Carolyn	Bugsy Goes to Galway	1 85371 147 0	£3.99
Swift Carolyn	Irish Myths and Tales	1 85371 103 9	£2.99
Swift Carolyn	Robbers on TV	1 85371 033 4	£2.99
Swift Carolyn	Robbers on the Streets	1 85371 113 6	£3.50
Traynor Shaun	A Little Man in England	1 85371 032 6	£2.99
Traynor Shaun	Hugo O'Huge	1 85371 048 2	£2.99
Traynor Shaun	The Giants' Olympics	1 85371 088 1	£2.99
Traynor Shaun	The Lost City of Belfast	1 85371 164 0	£3.50
	The Ultimate Children's Joke Book	1 85371 168 3	£2.99

While every effort is made to keep prices low, it is sometimes necessary to increase prices at short notice. Poolbeg Press Ltd reserves the right to show new retail prices on covers which may differ from those previously advertised in the text or elsewhere.

All Poolbeg books are available at your bookshop or newsagent or can be ordered from:

Poolbeg Press Knocksedan House
Forrest Great Swords Co Dublin
Tel: 01 407433 Fax: 01 403753

Please send a cheque or postal order (no currency) made payable to Poolbeg Press Ltd.

Allow 80p for postage for the first book, plus 50p for each additional book ordered.

Children's
POOLBEG

To get regular
information about
our books and authors join

THE POOLBEG
BOOK CLUB

To become a member of
THE POOLBEG BOOK CLUB
Write to Anne O'Reilly,
The Poolbeg Book Club,
Knocksedan House,
Swords, Co. Dublin.
Please write clearly and make sure to include
all the following details: Name, full address,
date of birth, school.